PETER S. BEAGLE is the magician we all apprenticed ourselves to. Before all the endless series and shared-world novels, Beagle was there to show us the amazing possibilities waiting in the worlds of fantasy, and he is still one of the masters by which the rest of the field is measured. I envy people reading these stories for the first time.
— *Lisa Goldstein*

Peter S. Beagle is (in no particular order) a wonderful writer, a fine human being, and a bandit prince out to steal readers' hearts.
— *Tad Williams*

Beagle would be one of the century's great writers in any arena he chose; we readers must feel blessed that Beagle picked fantasy as a homeland. Magic pumps like blood through the veins of his stories. Imparting passionately breathing, singing, laughing reality to the marvelous is his great gift to us all.
— *Edward Bryant*

...one of my favorite writers.
— *Madeleine L'Engle*

Peter S. Beagle illuminates with his own particular magic such commonplace matters as ghosts, unicorns, and werewolves. For years a loving readership has consulted him as an expert on those hearts' reasons that reason does not know.
— *Ursula K. LeGuin*

D1571728

The Rhinoceros Who Quoted Nietzsche and Other Odd Acquaintances is a retrospective collection of works by Peter S. Beagle, one of America's greatest living writers and fantasists. Originally published in 1997, this new edition makes the book widely available for the first time and contains an original preface by the author.

Beagle wrote his first novel, *A Fine and Private Place*, when he was only nineteen. Still in print today, this extraordinary tale of life, death, and all-too-human love launched him on a literary career which quickly expanded to include commissions for major magazines, Hollywood screenplays, and the unique novels and nonfiction works that have made him a favorite of millions of readers worldwide. He is a two-time winner of the Mythopoeic Award, for his novels *The Folk of the Air* and *Tamsin*, and in 1993 his dazzling *The Innkeeper's Song* won the Locus Award for Best Fantasy Novel of the year. In 1998 his short story "Come Lady Death" (included in this collection) was elected by members of SFWA to the Fantasy Hall of Fame. His most beloved novel, *The Last Unicorn*, was an underground bestseller when first released in 1968 and has been captivating audiences for decades; it is now acknowledged as a true classic in its field. An animated feature based on the book was released in 1982 and a new live-action version is in the works.

Peter S. Beagle

For Andrew Dwyer —

The Rhinoceros
Who Quoted Nietzsche

and other odd acquaintances

Peter S. Beagle

Peter S. Beagle

The Rhinoceros Who Quoted Nietzsche

and other odd acquaintances

Tachyon Publications
San Francisco, California

THE RHINOCEROS WHO QUOTED NIETZSCHE
and other odd acquaintances

Cover illustration by Michael Dashow
Typography by Ann Monn

TACHYON PUBLICATIONS
1459 18TH STREET #139
SAN FRANCISCO, CA 94107
(415) 285-5615

Edited by Jacob Weisman

ISBN: 1-892391-09-0

First Edition: December 1997

2nd Printing: September 1998

3rd Printing: September 2003

Printed in the United States of America by Phoenix Color Corporation

0   9   8   7   6   5   4   3

Permissions

for my mother,
Rebecca Soyer Beagle,
who told me stories,
and never thought I was weird

Table of Contents

PREFACE:
ON LOOKING BACK

Okay — seems there's this hairy old hillbilly and this little old Jew guy, and they walk into this bar together, and the bartender says....

No, that's not at all the way to start this thing, what possessed you? This is a Preface, fool — a preamble to a forty-year sampling of your work: a serious, measured assessment of where you've been and where you imagine going in the time left to you. And just because you've told stories and dumb jokes all your life, that doesn't mean —

And, see, these two old guys, this hillbilly and this old Jew, they haven't gotten together for a real long time, I forgot to mention that....

Look, quit it, okay? Just knock it off. Yeah, all right — you're just back from two days of racketing around the hills and coal mines and legendary labor battlefields of Eastern Kentucky with your old buddy Gurney Norman, and the pair of you hadn't seen each other for twenty-six years or so, and you couldn't stop talking and singing and laughing and reminiscing, even when looking at model churches, miniature wells and thousand-piece dollhouses by the roadside — what's all that got to do with your career, with a measured assessment and like that? This is a chance to appraise, and review, and evaluate; this is Liddychoor, as a man named Avram Davidson always used to call it. You get your elderly ass back to Liddychoor right now.

But that's just the trouble. I haven't aspired to being Liddychoor probably since Gurney and I met in a writing class at Stanford University in 1960. Gurney was twenty-three, straight out of Hazard, Kentucky, the son and grandson of miners. I was a wide-eyed Bronx twenty-one, quite well-read, and infinitely less hip than today's average nine-year-old. The class included Ken Kesey, Larry McMurtry, Joanna Ostrow, Chris Koch and James Baker Hall. Whatever else came of that

11

year, I know that it cured me forever of certain fantasies, certain great expectations, and any ambitions beyond telling the peculiar stories that were mine to tell the best way I could, just as Gurney was already telling his Kentucky stories, by turns deadpan hilarious and abruptly heart-squeezing. I didn't learn what I was at Stanford, or what I was meant to write, but I did learn what I wasn't, and what I couldn't ever do. And one of the things I definitely couldn't do — I really did understand it that early — was Liddychoor.

So anyway, they go to the racetrack, this old Jew and the old hillbilly — they've both got these white beards, did I say that? — and the Jew bets five bucks on a horse, first time in his life, and he wins nineteen-fifty. Now the hillbilly, he bets on a different horse, and he loses, so then the old Jew asks him how come he didn't bet on the same horse he did. And the hillbilly says, "Man, I ain't about winning. I'm about losing as little as possible."

Actually, we never walked into any bars during those two days together — you can't get beer in Kentucky on a Sunday, for one thing; and for another, Gurney had thoughtfully brought along a lot of Guinness, which we drank sitting in the car, keeping our hands well down between slugs, so as not to be noticed by passersby. But we did talk a lot, far more than we'd ever done in the old days, about our secret histories, both personal and artistic; and I know that somewhere in there I quoted the great Satchel Paige's immortal admonition, "Never look back. Something might be gaining on you." Gurney already knew that one, of course. He would.

The Rhinoceros Who Quoted Nietzsche represents — in far more than a literary sense — my own bewildering, rather off-center past. Browsing through these tales and articles I wrote so impossibly long ago, I catch glimpses — no, more than glimpses: bloody exposés and exhibitions — of the person Gurney met in the Jones Room at Stanford, the person I was, and have been, and still am, only now with the white beard and certain aches and scars and sorrows I don't remember acquiring…Yes, I do, I make sure I do, every one. An artist never knows what grief or guilt might some day come in useful.

So then the old hillbilly, he says to the Jew, "People calling you a cult writer these days — that's all I hear every time your name comes up. What on earth's a cult writer?" And the old Jew, he says back, "That's when your fans are just crazy about your stuff, only they got no money, so they get the books out of the library and read them over and over. Xerox them sometimes."

So the old hillbilly says, "Be damned, I'm a cult writer myself. Who knew?"

For the original publication of this book, I provided introductions to the sections containing my earliest published stories ("Come Lady Death" comes out of that Stanford class) and the freelance magazine work that fed my young family during the 1960s. I have no notion today why I wrote nothing about the five stories that might be considered the beginning of my Mature Period by people who consider such things. I remain quite fond of them all, especially the two most recent: "Julie's Unicorn," which brought back my old alter-ego Joe Farrell, and "Professor Gottesman and the Indian Rhinoceros," which may be the best short story I'll ever write. "The Naga," based on a Cambodian legend, was written for a book meant to accompany a public-television project which I still think was a great idea, but which never got on its feet, let alone off the ground. The plan was to create a mock-newscast series, with the first-century Roman naturalist Pliny the Elder as its anchorman. The Pliny the Elder Report would focus on breaking stories about mythological beings: griffins annually plaguing Central Asian tribes, sea-dragons drastically affecting the weather in China and Japan, scandalous doings off the Eddystone Light during the mermaid mating season. The book publisher folded; the producer became an eminent professor of journalism; nothing ever got written but "The Naga." It still matters a good deal to me, for a lot of reasons that don't matter here.

Then the old Jew, he tells the hillbilly, "You know, I envied you something fierce in those days, you and Larry and Ken and Jim. You had real roots in this country, you'd all been in Texas, Oregon, Kentucky for generations — you knew who you were and where you were from, and you could draw on that like an endless bank account. Me, I've always, always felt I was from another planet, some way — I had to create worlds to be from, if that makes any sense. We out of Guinness?"

Old hillbilly, he answers, "Two left. Finish up, and I'll show you something."

At sixty-four, I do still allow myself one grand vision, which is that the good times are just ahead. No backward glances, enough with all these scales and finger exercises — here comes the real stuff, here come the books I've been teaching myself to write since I was a child scrawling imitation Tarzan stories in the back row of my second-grade class. Here comes, at last, that weird old Chinese legend about the Yellow Emperor and the Mirror people; or maybe here should come first that big picaresque thing about the Spanish woman spy in Elizabethan England? Then there's that entire novel I wrote in 1961 and buried for over forty years — might just be salvageable, that one, with a whole lot of work. Or what about that mysterious fragment called "The Hunted" — at Stanford, was that? or even earlier, in the Malaga *pensione*, on whose borrowed typewriter? I have no smallest memory of writing that thing; would it be at all possible to find my way back into that shy, maladroit kid who must have had *something* in mind, so long ago? And even if I could, even if I could...

For all the talking we did, Gurney and I, during those two days on the road, what was left unsaid was the understanding that both of us are finally too old to concern ourselves with the image in the rear-view mirror. I can't speak for Gurney, but I bump into enough stuff when I'm looking straight ahead.

So anyway, this old hillbilly and this old Jew, they walk over this railroad bridge across a kind of muddy little creek, and the hillbilly, he stops midway and he points way down toward the far bank. And there's this bunch of kids, maybe eight, nine, ten years old, whatever, and they're playing in the mud, in the water, fishing and such. And the hillbilly, he says to the Jew, "That's me. That is me down there, that's exactly where I played when I was their age. You're looking straight back down through time at me."

We waved. You don't look back — Satchel was quite right about that — but you do wave. It's a good thing to wave. A couple of the kids waved up at us, but most of them were too occupied with the moment, with their lives. We stood there for some while before we walked on.

— Peter S. Beagle
Oakland, California
May 2003

Under the Zucchini
by Patricia A. McKillup

Recently, searching through my books for something else entirely, I came across an anthology titled *The Seventh World Fantasy Convention*. It is a collection of short pieces by various fantasy writers who came, or at least offered a tale to, the World Fantasy Convention held in Berkeley, California, in 1981. I can't remember now why I opened it — maybe to see what of mine was published in it — but I actually found what might be called a piece of literary obscura. It's a lovely series of poems by Peter, written for children, and inspired by the Unicorn Tapestries hanging in the Cloisters of New York City. They were not bought by the publisher who asked him to write them; beyond publication in the WFC collection, I don't know if they ever again saw the light of day. But it was a wonderful thing to find on my shelves: early Peter Beagle, who could write such things as "the air like honey and harps and snow" and who still does.

Rereading "Lila the Werewolf" after many years, I was astonished again and again by metaphors, by crazed juxtapositions and unexpected rhythms:

"The terrible eyes of a herald angel stricken dumb. . ."

"Standing in broccoli, in black taffeta, with a front like a ferryboat. . ."

"Down to the realms where the great dim water mains roll like whales, and the gas lines hump and preen. . ."

"The full moon skidded down the sky, thinning like a tatter of butter in a skillet. . ."

And this is just the early work! In his introduction to *The Fantasy Worlds of Peter Beagle*, published by Viking Press in 1978, Peter seems apologetic about various things in the story: gore, domineering mothers, rampaging female werewolves. But the writing itself transcends its subject; he draws us from image to image, taking poetry from the ridiculous, the dangerous, the familiar and the forgotten details and underpinnings of a city he loved. It's a dark and very funny tale; a glimpse of the world through the young author's eyes, thirty years ago.

Farrell, the narrator, returns to us again in "Julie's Unicorn," still as prone as ever to attracting women with odd talents, and animals out of the realms of fantasy.

He is older now, like the author, perhaps wiser, but he exists in the same unpredictable world where secret notes are dispatched under the zucchini and mythical beasts take up residence under the water cooler. This tale, colored with the pastels of the California sky, flavored with mangoes rather than blood, flows with the same energetic precision of language; the storyteller may have weathered, but his tools are as bright as ever.

I can't remember exactly when I first met Peter. Back when we were both a lot younger, that much I know, and probably at a convention or a librarians' conference; possibly in a book store where I brought a novel of his to be signed. I know that I once possessed a first edition of *The Last Unicorn*, hot off the press, and I believe that, by the time I lost it, it had been signed by the author. Twenty years or so ago, that would be, give or take a year. I lived for a year (not the one given or taken) in a small coastal town in California called Aptos. At that time, Peter was living on a farm farther south in Watsonville, writing in a barn with a pet ferret in his pocket. I remember, going to visit him there, meeting a dog who was part wolf, very pretty and very shy. Every blue moon or so, Peter and I would get together for beer and a chat about books or shop. In those days, he sang on Saturday nights in a tiny restaurant in Santa Cruz: French songs, the likes of which I'd never heard before, that sounded romantic and cynical and never seemed to have happy endings. After I moved away, we continued, through the years, to run across one another at fantasy conventions. Or I would bring friends to hear him play. Or he would visit me, and play his music in my living room, as he did here in New York, not very long ago, charming his friends and family once again, and bringing a touch of elegance to a cold autumn evening in the Catskills. Peter charms in life as well as in art; like the Ancient Mariner, he fixes you with his glittering eye and induces in you a sort of cat-like contentment as he speaks; his voice could make music of the ingredients off a cereal box.

I have read all his books through the years, including perhaps the strangest: *I See By My Outfit*. The paperback jacket for that had the author on the front, in garish color, perched on a motorcycle and managing to look patient and ethereal and resigned at the same time, as though he would, if you didn't mind, rather be anywhere else but there. I've listened to him read his own work; I've seen the movie made of *The Last Unicorn*, and awaited, like many others of my generation, the movie of *The Lord of the Rings*, for which he and Chris Conklin wrote the screenplay. That, I recall, was the best thing about the movie. If a novel or a story or a reading announcement said Peter Beagle on it, I was simply drawn to it, with a kind of mindless conviction, the way you are drawn to chocolate or to Yosemite Falls, knowing that you are about to achieve a state of pleasure. Even Peter being absent-minded at his craft, or not fully inspired, can be a treat; there is always the word-play, the skewed detail, the character springing full-blown out of nowhere, like the grandmother in *The Unicorn Sonata*, stubborn, wise, endearing.

In "Professor Gottesman and the Indian Rhinoceros" the strands connecting Peter's short fiction shine clearly: love, death, transformation, humor, wonder. Death might be a lovely young woman or a unicorn; love comes to dry old professors and to cynical aristocrats; one might find a rhinoceros at the tea-table or a wolf in the bed and learn to live with the mystery. I am now reading his most recent work: a set of stories titled *Giant Bones*. I thought that, after all these years, I couldn't be surprised: this book would be like that one with the talking butterfly, or maybe the one over there with the ghosts chatting in the cemetery. Or maybe like the one where the woman turns into a man in the middle. But no. The voice that begins the first tale belongs to someone I've never met before, raucous, ungainly, the most unlikely heroine. Her voice is her own; the style, like gold melting over gravel, fluid and full of surprises, is the best of a master storyteller.

PETER S. BEAGLE

STORIES

PETER S. BEAGLE

Professor Gottesman
and the Indian Rhinoceros

Professor Gustave Gottesman went to a zoo for the first time when he was thirty-four years old. There is an excellent zoo in Zurich, which was Professor Gottesman's birthplace, and where his sister still lived, but Professor Gottesman had never been there. From an early age he had determined on the study of philosophy as his life's work; and for any true philosopher this world is zoo enough, complete with cages, feeding times, breeding programs, and earnest docents, of which he was wise enough to know that he was one. Thus, the first zoo he ever saw was the one in the middle-sized Midwestern American city where he worked at a middle-sized university, teaching Comparative Philosophy in comparative contentment. He was tall and rather thin, with a round, undistinguished face, a snub nose, a random assortment of sandy-ish hair, and a pair of very intense and very distinguished brown eyes that always seemed to be looking a little deeper than they meant to, embarrassing the face around them no end. His students and colleagues were quite fond of him, in an indulgent sort of way.

And how did the good Professor Gottesman happen at last to visit a zoo? It came about in this way: his older sister Edith came from Zurich to stay with him for several weeks, and she brought her daughter, his niece Nathalie, along with her. Nathalie was seven, both in years, and in the number of her there sometimes seemed to be, for the Professor had never been used to children even when he was one. She was a generally pleasant little girl, though, as far as he could tell; so when his sister besought him to spend one of his free afternoons with Nathalie while she went to lunch and a gallery opening with an old friend, the Professor graciously consented. And Nathalie wanted very much to go to the zoo and see tigers.

"So you shall," her uncle announced gallantly. "Just as soon as I find out exactly where the zoo is." He consulted with his best friend, a fat, cheerful, harmonica-playing professor of medieval Italian poetry named Sally Lowry, who had known him long and well enough (she was the only person in the world who called him Gus) to draw an elaborate two-colored map of the route, write out very precise directions beneath it, and make several copies of this document, in case of accidents. Thus equipped, and accompanied by Charles, Nathalie's stuffed bedtime tiger, whom she desired to introduce to his grand cousins, they set off together for the zoo on a gray, cool spring afternoon. Professor Gottesman quoted Thomas Hardy to Nathalie, improvising a German translation for her benefit as he went along.

> This is the weather the cuckoo likes,
> And so do I;
> When showers betumble the chestnut spikes,
> And nestlings fly.

"Charles likes it too," Nathalie said. "It makes his fur feel all sweet."

They reached the zoo without incident, thanks to Professor Lowry's excellent map, and Professor Gottesman bought Nathalie a bag of something sticky, unhealthy, and forbidden, and took her straight off to see the tigers. Their hot, meaty smell and their lightning-colored eyes were a bit too much for him, and so he sat on a bench nearby and watched Nathalie perform the introductions for Charles. When she came back to Professor Gottesman, she told him that Charles had been very well-behaved, as had all the tigers but one, who was rudely indifferent. "He was probably just visiting," she said. "A tourist or something." The Professor was still marveling at the amount of contempt one small girl could infuse into the word tourist, when he heard a voice, sounding almost at his shoulder, say, "Why, Professor Gottesman — how nice to see you at last." It was a low voice, a bit hoarse, with excellent diction, speaking good Zurich German with a very slight, unplaceable accent.

Professor Gottesman turned quickly, half-expecting to see some old acquaintance from home, whose name he would inevitably have forgotten. Such embarrassments were altogether too common in his gently preoccupied life. His friend Sally Lowry once observed, "We see each other just about every day, Gus, and I'm still not sure you really recognize me. If I wanted to hide from you, I'd just change my hairstyle."

There was no one at all behind him. The only thing he saw was the rutted, muddy rhinoceros yard, for some reason placed directly across from the big cats' cages. The one rhinoceros in residence was standing by the fence, torpidly mumbling a mouthful of moldy-looking hay. It was an Indian rhinoceros, according to the placard on the gate: as big as the Professor's compact car, and the approximate color of old cement. The creaking slabs of its skin smelled of stale urine, and it had only one horn, caked with sticky mud. Flies buzzed around its small, heavy-lidded eyes, which regarded Professor Gottesman with immense, ancient unconcern. But there was no other person in the vicinity who might have addressed him.

Professor Gottesman shook his head, scratched it, shook it again, and turned back to the tigers. But the voice came again. "Professor, it was indeed I who spoke. Come and talk to me, if you please."

No need, surely, to go into Professor Gottesman's reaction: to describe in detail how he gasped, turned pale, and looked wildly around for any corroborative witness. It is worth mentioning, however, that at no time did he bother to splutter the requisite splutter in such cases: "My God, I'm either dreaming, drunk, or crazy." If he was indeed just as classically absent-minded and impractical as everyone who knew him agreed, he was also more of a realist than many of them. This is generally true of philosophers, who tend, as a group, to be on terms of mutual respect with the impossible. Therefore, Professor Gottesman did the only proper thing under the circumstances. He introduced his niece Nathalie to the rhinoceros.

Nathalie, for all her virtues, was not a philosopher, and could not hear the rhinoceros's gracious greeting. She was, however, seven years old, and a well-brought-up seven-year-old has no difficulty with the notion that a rhinoceros — or a goldfish, or a coffee table — might be able to talk; nor in accepting that some people can hear coffee-table speech and some people cannot. She said a polite hello to the rhinoceros, and then became involved in her own conversation with stuffed Charles, who apparently had a good deal to say about tigers.

"A mannerly child," the rhinoceros commented. "One sees so few here. Most of them throw things."

His mouth was dry, and his voice shaky but contained, Professor Gottesman asked carefully, "Tell me, if you will — can all rhinoceri speak, or only the Indian species?" He wished furiously that he had thought to bring along his notebook.

"I have no idea," the rhinoceros answered him candidly. "I myself, as it happens, am a unicorn."

Professor Gottesman wiped his balding forehead. "Please," he said earnestly. "Please. A rhinoceros, even a rhinoceros that speaks, is as real a creature as I. A unicorn, on the other hand, is a being of pure fantasy, like mermaids, or dragons, or the chimera. I consider very little in this universe as absolutely, indisputably certain, but I would feel so much better if you could see your way to being merely a talking rhinoceros. For my sake, if not your own."

It seemed to the Professor that the rhinoceros chuckled slightly, but it might only have been a ruminant's rumbling stomach. "My Latin designation is *Rhinoceros unicornis*," the great animal remarked. "You may have noticed it on the sign."

Professor Gottesman dismissed the statement as brusquely as he would have if the rhinoceros had delivered it in class. "Yes, yes, yes, and the manatee, which suckles its young erect in the water and so gave rise to the myth of the mermaid, is assigned to the order *sirenia*. Classification is not proof."

"And proof," came the musing response, "is not necessarily truth. You look at me and see a rhinoceros, because I am not white, not graceful, far from beautiful, and my horn is no elegant spiral but a bludgeon of matted hair. But suppose that you had grown up expecting a unicorn to look and behave and smell exactly as I do — would not the rhinoceros then be the legend? Suppose that everything you believed about unicorns — everything except the way they look — were true of me? Consider the possibilities, Professor, while you push the remains of that bun under the gate."

Professor Gottesman found a stick and poked the grimy bit of pastry — about the same shade as the rhinoceros, it was — where the creature could wrap a prehensile upper lip around it. He said, somewhat tentatively, "Very well. The unicorn's horn was supposed to be an infallible guide to detecting poisons."

"The most popular poisons of the Middle Ages and Renaissance," replied the rhinoceros, "were alkaloids. Pour one of those into a goblet made of compressed hair, and see what happens." It belched resoundingly, and Nathalie giggled.

Professor Gottesman, who was always invigorated by a good

argument with anyone, whether colleague, student, or rhinoceros, announced, "Isidore of Seville wrote in the seventh century that the unicorn was a cruel beast, that it would seek out elephants and lions to fight with them. Rhinoceri are equally known for their fierce, aggressive nature, which often leads them to attack anything that moves in their shortsighted vision. What have you to say to that?"

"Isidore of Seville," said the rhinoceros thoughtfully, "was a most learned man, much like your estimable self, who never saw a rhinoceros in his life, or an elephant either, being mainly preoccupied with church history and canon law. I believe he did see a lion at some point. If your charming niece is quite done with her snack?"

"She is not, " Professor Gottesman answered, "and do not change the subject. If you are indeed a unicorn, what are you doing scavenging dirty buns and candy in this public establishment? It is an article of faith that a unicorn can only be taken by a virgin, in whose innocent embrace the ferocious creature becomes meek and docile. Are you prepared to tell me that you were captured under such circumstances?"

The rhinoceros was silent for some little while before it spoke again. "I cannot," it said judiciously, "vouch for the sexual history of the gentleman in the baseball cap who fired a tranquilizer dart into my left shoulder. I would, however, like to point out that the young of our species on occasion become trapped in vines and slender branches which entangle their horns — and the Latin for such branches is *virge*. What Isidore of Seville made of all this. . ." It shrugged, which is difficult for a rhinoceros, and a remarkable thing to see.

"Sophistry," said the Professor, sounding unpleasantly beleaguered even in his own ears. "Casuistry. Semantics. Chop-logic. The fact remains, a rhinoceros is and a unicorn isn't." This last sounds much more impressive in German. "You will excuse me," he went on, "but we have other specimens to visit, do we not, Nathalie?"

"No," Nathalie said. "Charles and I just wanted to see the tigers."

"Well, we have seen the tigers," Professor Gottesman said through his teeth. "And I believe it's beginning to rain, so we will go home now." He took Nathalie's hand firmly and stood up, as that obliging child snuggled Charles firmly under her arm and bobbed a demure European curtsy to the rhinoceros. It bent its head to her, the mud-thick horn almost brushing the ground. Professor Gottesman, mildest of men, snatched her away.

"Good-bye, Professor," came the hoarse, placid voice behind

him. "I look forward to our next meeting." The words were somewhat muffled, because Nathalie had tossed the remainder of her sticky snack into the yard as her uncle hustled her off. Professor Gottesman did not turn his head. Driving home through the rain — which had indeed begun to fall, though very lightly — the Professor began to have an indefinably uneasy feeling that caused him to spend more time peering at the rear-view mirror than in looking properly ahead. Finally, he asked Nathalie, "Please, would you and — ah — you and Charles climb into the backseat and see whether we are being followed?"

Nathalie was thrilled. "Like in the spy movies?" She jumped to obey, but reported after a few minutes of crouching on the seat that she could detect nothing out of the ordinary. "I saw a helicopiter," she told him, attempting the English word. "Charles thinks they might be following us that way, but I don't know. Who is spying on us, Uncle Gustave?"

"No one, no one," Professor Gottesman answered. "Never mind, child, I am getting silly in America. It happens, never mind." But a few moments later the curious apprehension was with him again, and Nathalie was happily occupied for the rest of the trip home in scanning the traffic behind them through an imaginary periscope, yipping "It's that one!" from time to time, and being invariably disappointed when another prime suspect turned off down a side street. When they reached Professor Gottesman's house, she sprang out of the car immediately, ignoring her mother's welcome until she had checked under all four fenders for possible homing devices. "Bugs," she explained importantly to the two adults. "That was Charles's idea. Charles would make a good spy, I think."

She ran inside, leaving Edith to raise her fine eyebrows at her brother. Professor Gottesman said heavily, "We had a nice time. Don't ask." And Edith, being a wise older sister, left it at that.

The rest of the visit was enjoyably uneventful. The Professor went to work according to his regular routine, while his sister and his niece explored the city, practiced their English together, and cooked Swiss-German specialties to surprise him when he came home. Nathalie never asked to go to the zoo again — stuffed Charles having lately shown an interest in international intrigue — nor did she ever mention that her uncle had formally introduced her to a rhinoceros and spent part of an afternoon sitting on a bench arguing with it. Professor Gottesman was genuinely sorry when she and Edith left for Zurich, which rather surprised him. He hardly ever missed people, or thought much about anyone who was not actually present.

It rained again on the evening that they went to the airport. Returning alone, the Professor was startled, and a bit disquieted, to see large muddy footprints on his walkway and his front steps. They were, as nearly as he could make out, the marks of a three-toed foot, having a distinct resemblance to the ace of clubs in a deck of cards. The door was locked and bolted, as he had left it, and there was no indication of any attempt to force and entry. Professor Gottesman hesitated, looked quickly around him, and went inside.

The rhinoceros was in the living room, lying peacefully on its side before the artificial fireplace — which was lit — like a very large dog. It opened one eye as he entered and greeted him politely. "Welcome home, Professor. You will excuse me, I hope, if I do not rise?"

Professor Gottesman's legs grew weak under him. He groped blindly for a chair, found it, fell into it, his face white and freezing cold. He managed to ask, "How — how did you get in here?" in a small, faraway voice.

"The same way I got out of the zoo," the rhinoceros answered him. "I would have come sooner, but with your sister and your niece already here, I thought my presence might make things perhaps a little too crowded for you. I do hope their departure went well." It yawned widely and contentedly, showing blunt, fist-sized teeth and a gray-pink tongue like a fish fillet.

"I must telephone the zoo," Professor Gottesman whispered. "Yes, of course, I will call the zoo." But he did not move from the chair.

The rhinoceros shook its head as well as it could in a prone position. "Oh, I wouldn't bother with that, truly. It will only distress them if anyone learns that they have mislaid a creature as large as I am. And they will never believe that I am in your house. Take my word for it, there will be no mention of my having left their custody. I have some experience in these matters." It yawned again and closed its eyes. "Excellent fireplace you have," it murmured drowsily. "I think I shall lie exactly here every night. Yes, I do think so."

And it was asleep, snoring with the rhythmic roar and fading whistle of a fast freight crossing a railroad bridge. Professor Gottesman sat staring in his chair for a long time before he managed to stagger to the telephone in the kitchen.

Sally Lowry came over early the next morning, as she had promised several times before the Professor would let her off the phone. She took one quick look at him as she entered and said briskly, "Well, whatever came to dinner, you look as though it got the bed and you slept on the living room floor."

"I did not sleep at all," Professor Gottesman informed her grimly. "Come with me, please, Sally, and you shall see why."

But the rhinoceros was not in front of the fireplace, where it had still been lying when the Professor came downstairs. He looked around for it increasingly frantic, saying over and over, "It was just here, it has been here all night. Wait, wait, Sally, I will show you. Wait only a moment."

For he had suddenly heard the unmistakable gurgle of water in the pipes overhead. He rushed up the narrow hairpin stairs (his house was, as the real-estate agent had put it, "an old charmer") and burst into his bathroom, blinking through the clouds of steam to find the rhinoceros lolling blissfully in the tub, its nose barely above water and its hind legs awkwardly sticking straight up in the air. There were puddles all over the floor.

"Good morning," the rhinoceros greeted Professor Gottesman. "I could wish your facilities a bit larger, but the hot water is splendid, pure luxury. We never had hot baths at the zoo."

"Get out of my tub!" the Professor gabbled, coughing and wiping his face. "You will get out of my tub this instant!"

The rhinoceros remained unruffled. "I am not sure I can. Not just like that. It's rather a complicated affair."

"Get out exactly the way you got in!" shouted Professor Gottesman. "How did you get up here at all? I never heard you on the stairs."

"I tried not to disturb you," the rhinoceros said meekly. "Unicorns can move very quietly when we need to."

"*Out!*" the Professor thundered. He had never thundered before, and it made his throat hurt. "Out of my bathtub, out of my house! And clean up that floor before you go!"

He stormed back down the stairs to meet a slightly anxious Sally Lowry waiting at the bottom. "What was all that yelling about?" she wanted to know. "You're absolutely pink — it's sort of sweet, actually. Are you all right?"

"Come up with me," Professor Gottesman demanded. "Come right now." He seized his friend by the wrist and practically dragged her into his bathroom, where there was no sign of the rhinoceros. The tub was empty and dry, the floor was spotlessly clean; the air smelled faintly of tile cleaner. Professor Gottesman stood gaping in the doorway, muttering over and over, "But it was here. It was in the tub."

"What was in the tub?" Sally asked. The Professor took a long, deep breath and turned to face her.

"A rhinoceros," he said. "It says it's a unicorn, but it is nothing but an Indian rhinoceros." Sally's mouth opened, but no sound came out. Professor Gottesman said, "It followed me home."

Fortunately, Sally Lowry was not more concerned with the usual splutters of denial and disbelief than was the Professor himself. She closed her mouth, caught her own breath, and said, "Well, any rhinoceros that could handle those stairs, wedge itself into that skinny tub of yours, and tidy up afterwards would have to be a unicorn. Obvious. Gus, I don't care what time it is, I think you need a drink."

Professor Gottesman recounted his visit to the zoo with Nathalie, and all that had happened thereafter, while Sally rummaged through his minimally stocked liquor cabinet and mixed what she called a "Lowry Land Mine." It calmed the Professor only somewhat, but it did at least restore his coherency. He said earnestly, "Sally, I don't know how it talks. I don't know how it escaped from the zoo, or found its way here, or how it got into my house and my bathtub, and I am afraid to imagine where it is now. But the creature is an Indian rhinoceros, the sign said so. It is simply not possible — not possible — that is could be a unicorn."

"Sounds like *Harvey*," Sally mused. Professor Gottesman stared at her. "You know, the play about the guy who's buddies with an invisible white rabbit. A big white rabbit."

"But this one is not invisible!" the Professor cried. "People at the zoo, they saw it — Nathalie saw it. It bowed to her, quite courteously."

"Um," Sally said. "Well, I haven't seen it yet, but I live in hope. Meanwhile, you've got a class, and I've got office hours. Want me to make you another Land Mine?"

Professor Gottesman shuddered slightly. "I think not. We are discussing today how Fichte and von Schelling's work leads us to Hegel, and I need my wits about me. Thank you for coming to my house, Sally. You are a good friend. Perhaps I really am suffering from delusions, after all. I think I would almost prefer it so."

"Not me," Sally said. "I'm getting a unicorn out of this, if it's the last thing I do." She patted his arm. "You're more fun than a barrel of MFA candidates, Gus, and you're also the only gentleman I've ever met. I don't know what I'd do for company around here without you."

Professor Gottesman arrived early for his seminar on "The Heirs of Kant." There was no one in the classroom when he entered, except for the rhinoceros. It had plainly already attempted to sit on one of the chairs, which lay in splinters on the floor. Now it was warily eyeing a ragged hassock near the coffee machine.

"What are you doing here?" Professor Gottesman fairly screamed at it.

"Only auditing," the rhinoceros answered. "I thought it might be rewarding to see you at work. I promise not to say a word."

Professor Gottesman pointed to the door. He had opened his mouth to order the rhinoceros, once and for all, out of his life, when two of his students walked into the room. The Professor closed his mouth, gulped, greeted his students, and ostentatiously began to examine his lecture notes, mumbling professorial mumbles to himself, while the rhinoceros, unnoticed, negotiated a kind of armed truce with the hassock. True to its word, it listened in attentive silence all through the seminar, though Professor Gottesman had an uneasy moment when it seemed about to be drawn into a heated debate over the precise nature of von Schelling's intellectual debt to the von Schlegel brothers. He was so desperately careful not to let the rhinoceros catch his eye that he never noticed until the last student had left that the beast was gone, too. None of the class had even once commented on its presence; except for the shattered chair, there was no indication that it had ever been there.

Professor Gottesman drove slowly home in a disorderly state of mind. On the one hand, he wished devoutly never to see the rhinoceros again; on the other, he could not help wondering exactly when it had left the classroom. "Was it displeased with my summation of the *Ideas for a Philosophy of Nature*?" he said aloud in the car. "Or perhaps it was something I said during the argument about *Die Weltalter*. Granted, I have never been entirely comfortable with that book, but I do not recall saying anything exceptionable." Hearing himself justifying his interpretations to a rhinoceros, he slapped his own cheek very hard and drove the rest of the way with the car radio tuned to the loudest, ugliest music he could find.

The rhinoceros was dozing before the fireplace as before, but lumbered clumsily to a sitting position as soon as he entered the living room. "Bravo Professor!" it cried in plainly genuine enthusiasm. "You were absolutely splendid. It was an honor to be present at your seminar."

The Professor was furious to realize that he was blushing; yet it was impossible to respond to such praise with an eviction notice. There was nothing for him to do but reply, a trifle stiffly, "Thank you, most gratifying." But the rhinoceros was clearly waiting for something more, and Professor Gottesman was, as his friend Sally had said, a gentleman. He went on, "You are welcome to audit the class again, if you like. We will be considering Rousseau next week, and then proceed through the romantic philosophers to Nietzsche and Schopenhauer."

"With a little time to spare for the American Transcendentalists, I should hope," suggested the rhinoceros. Professor Gottesman, being some distance past surprise, nodded. The rhinoceros said reflectively, "I think I should prefer to hear you on Comte and John Stuart Mill. The romantics always struck me as fundamentally unsound."

This position agreed so much with the Professor's own opinion that he found himself, despite himself, gradually warming toward the rhinoceros. Still formal, he asked, "May I perhaps offer you a drink? Some coffee or tea?"

"Tea would be very nice," the rhinoceros answered, "if you should happen to have a bucket." Professor Gottesman did not, and the rhinoceros told him not to worry about it. It settled back down before the fire, and the Professor drew up a rocking chair. The rhinoceros said, "I must admit, I do wish I could hear you speak on the scholastic philosophers. That's really my period, after all."

"I will be giving such a course next year," the Professor said, a little shyly. "It is to be a series of lectures on medieval Christian thought, beginning with St. Augustine and the Neoplatonists and ending with William of Occam. Possibly you could attend some of those talks."

The rhinoceros's obvious pleasure at the invitation touched Professor Gottesman surprisingly deeply. Even Sally Lowry, who often dropped in on his classes unannounced, did so, as he knew, out of affection for him, and not from any serious interest in epistemology or the Milesian School. He was beginning to wonder whether there might be a way to permit the rhinoceros to sample the cream sherry he kept aside for company, when the creature added, with a wheezy chuckle, "Of course, Augustine and the rest never did quite come to terms with such pagan survivals as unicorns. The best they could do was associate us with the Virgin Mary, and to suggest that our horns somehow represented the unity of Christ and his church. Bernard of Trèves even went so far as to identify Christ directly with the unicorn, but it was never a comfortable union. Spiral peg in square hole, so to speak."

Professor Gottesman was no more at ease with the issue than St. Augustine had been. But he was an honest person — only among philosophers is this considered part of the job description — and so he felt it his duty to say, "While I respect your intelligence and your obvious intellectual curiosity, none of this yet persuades me that you are in fact a unicorn. I still must regard you as an exceedingly learned and well-mannered Indian rhinoceros."

The rhinoceros took this in good part, saying, "Well, well, we will agree to disagree on that point for the time being. Although I certainly hope that you will let me know if you should need your drinking water purified." As before, and so often thereafter, Professor Gottesman could not be completely sure that the rhinoceros was joking. Dismissing the subject, it went on to ask, "But about the Scholastics — do you plan to discuss the later Thomist reformers at all? Saint Cajetan rather dominates the movement, to my mind; if he had any real equals, I'm afraid I can't recall them."

"Ah," said the Professor. They were up until five in the morning, and it was the rhinoceros who dozed off first. The question of the rhinoceros's leaving Professor Gottesman's house never came up again. It continued to sleep in the living room, for the most part, though on warm summer nights it had a fondness for the young willow tree that had been a Christmas present from Sally. Professor Gottesman never learned whether it was male or female, nor how it nourished its massive, noisy body, nor how it managed its toilet facilities — a reticent man himself, he respected reticence in others. As a houseguest, the rhinoceros's only serious fault was a continuing predilection for hot baths (with Epsom salts, when it could get them.) But it always cleaned up after itself, and was extremely conscientious about not tracking mud into the house; and it can be safely said that none of the Professor's visitors — even the rare ones who spent a night or two under his roof — ever remotely suspected that they were sharing living quarters with a rhinoceros. All in all, it proved to be a most discreet and modest beast.

The Professor had few friends, apart from Sally, and none whom he would have called on in a moment of bewildering crisis, as he had called on her. He avoided whatever social or academic gatherings he could reasonably avoid; as a consequence his evenings had generally been lonely ones, though he might not have called them so. Even if he had admitted the term, he would surely have insisted that there was nothing necessarily wrong with loneliness, in and of itself. "*I think*," he would have said — did often say, in fact, to Sally Lowry. "There are people, you know, for whom thinking is company, thinking is entertainment, parties, dancing even. The others, other people, they absolutely will not believe this."

"You're right," Sally said. "One thing about you, Gus, when you're right you're really right."

Now, however, the Professor could hardly wait for the time of day when, after a cursory dinner (he was an indifferent, impatient eater, and truly tasted little difference between a frozen dish and one that had taken half a day to prepare), he would pour himself a glass of wine and sit down in the living room to debate philosophy with a huge mortar-colored beast that always smelled vaguely incontinent, no matter how many baths it had taken that afternoon. Looking eagerly forward all day to anything was a new experience for him. It appeared to be the same for the rhinoceros.

As the animal had foretold, there was never the slightest suggestion in the papers or on television that the local zoo was missing one of its larger odd-toed ungulates. The Professor went there once or twice in great trepidation, convinced that he would be recognized and accused immediately of conspiracy in the rhinoceros's escape. But nothing of the sort happened. The yard where the rhinoceros had been kept was now occupied by a pair of despondent-looking African elephants; when Professor Gottesman made a timid inquiry of a guard, he was curtly informed that the zoo had never possessed a rhinoceros of any species. "Endangered species," the guard told him. "Too much red tape you have to go through to get one these days. Just not worth the trouble, mean as they are."

Professor Gottesman grew placidly old with the rhinoceros — that is to say, the Professor grew old, while the rhinoceros never changed in any way that he could observe. Granted, he was not the most observant of men, nor the most sensitive to change, except when threatened by it. Nor was he in the least ambitious: promotions and pay raises happened, when they happened, somewhere in the same cloudily benign middle distance as did those departmental meetings that he actually had to sit through. The companionship of the rhinoceros, while increasingly his truest delight, also became as much of a cozily reassuring habit as his classes, his office hours, the occasional dinner and movie or museum excursion with Sally Lowry, and the books on French and German philosophy that he occasionally published through the university press over the years. They were indifferently reviewed, and sold poorly.

"Which is undoubtedly as it should be," Professor Gottesman frequently told Sally when dropping her off at her house, well across town from his own. "I think I am a good teacher — that, yes — but I am decidedly not an original thinker, and I was never much of a writer even in German. It does no harm to say that I am not an exceptional man, Sally. It does not hurt me."

"I don't know what exceptional means to you or anyone else," Sally would answer stubbornly. "To me it means being unique, one of a kind, and that's definitely you, old Gus. I never thought you belonged in this town, or this university, or probably this century. But I'm surely glad you've been here."

Once in a while she might ask him casually how his unicorn was getting on these days. The Professor, who had long since accepted the fact that no one ever saw the rhinoceros unless it chose to be seen, invariably rose to the bait, saying, "It is no more a unicorn than it ever was, Sally, you know that." He would sip his latte in mild indignation, and eventually add, "Well, we will clearly never see eye to eye on the Vienna Circle, or the logical positivists in general — it is a very conservative creature, in some ways. But we did come to a tentative agreement about Bergson, last Thursday it was, so I would have to say that we are going along quite amiably."

Sally rarely pressed him further. Sharp-tongued, solitary, and profoundly irreverent, only with Professor Gottesman did she bother to know when to leave things alone. Most often, she would take out her battered harmonica and play one or another of his favorite tunes" — "Sweet Georgia Brown" or "Hurry on Down." He never sang along, but he always hummed and grunted and thumped his bony knees. Once he mentioned diffidently that the rhinoceros appeared to have a peculiar fondness for "Slow Boat to China." Sally pretended not to hear him.

In the appointed fullness of time, the university retired Professor Gottesman in a formal ceremony, attended by, among others, Sally Lowry, his sister Edith, all the way from Zurich, and the rhinoceros — the latter having spent all that day in the bathtub, in anxious preparation. Each of them assured him that he looked immensely distinguished as he was invested with the rank of *emeritus*, which allowed him to lecture as many as four times a year, and to be available to counsel promising graduate students when he chose. In addition, a special chair with his name on it was reserved exclusively for his use at the Faculty Club. He was quite proud of never once having sat in it.

"Strange, I am like a movie star now," he said to the rhinoceros. "You should see. Now I walk across the campus and the students line up, they line up to watch me totter past. I can hear their whispers — 'Here he comes!' 'There he goes!' Exactly the same ones they are who used to cut my classes because I bored them so. Completely absurd."

"Enjoy it as your due," the rhinoceros proposed. "You were entitled to their respect then — take pleasure in it now, however misplaced it may seem to you." But the Professor shook his head, smiling wryly.

"Do you know what kind of star I am really like?" he asked. "I am like the old, old star that died so long ago, so far away, that its last light is only reaching our eyes today. They fall in on themselves, you know, those dead stars, they go cold and invisible, even though we think we are seeing them in the night sky. That is just how I would be, if not for you. And for Sally, of course."

In fact, Professor Gottesman found little difficulty in making his peace with age and retirement. His needs were simple, his pension and savings adequate to meet them, and his health as sturdy as generations of Swiss peasant ancestors could make it. For the most part he continued to live as he always had, the one difference being that he now had more time for study, and could stay up as late as he chose arguing about structuralism with the rhinoceros, or listening to Sally Lowry reading her new translation of Calvalcanti or Frescobaldi. At first he attended every conference of philosophers to which he was invited, feeling a certain vague obligation to keep abreast of new thought in his field. This compulsion passed quickly, however, leaving him perfectly satisfied to have as little as possible to do with academic life, except when he needed to use the library. Sally once met him there for lunch to find him feverishly rifling the ten Loeb Classic volumes of Philo Judaeus. "We were debating the concept of the logos last night," he explained to her, "and then the impossible beast rampaged off on a tangent involving Philo's locating the roots of Greek philosophy in the Torah: Forgive me, Sally, but I may be here for awhile." Sally lunched alone that day.

The Professor's sister Edith died younger than she should have. He grieved for her, and took much comfort in the fact that Nathalie never failed to visit him when she came to America. The last few times, she had brought a husband and two children with her — the youngest hugging a ragged but indomitable tiger named Charles under his arm.

They most often swept him off for the evening; and it was on one such occasion, just after they had brought him home and said their good-byes, and their rented car had rounded the corner, that the mugging occurred.

Professor Gottesman was never quite sure himself about what actually took place. He remembered a light scuffle of footfalls, remembered a savage blow on the side of his head, then another impact as his cheek and forehead hit the ground. There were hands clawing through his pockets, low voices so distorted by obscene viciousness that he lost English completely, became for the first time in fifty years a terrified immigrant, once more unable to cry out for help in this new and dreadful country. A faceless figure billowed over him, grabbing his collar, pulling him close, mouthing words he could not understand. It was brandishing something menacingly in its free hand.

Then it vanished abruptly, as though blasted away by the sidewalk-shaking bellow of rage that was Professor Gottesman's last clear memory until he woke in a strange bed, with Sally Lowry, Nathalie, and several policemen bending over him. The next day's newspapers ran the marvelous story of a retired philosophy professor, properly frail and elderly, not only fighting off a pair of brutal muggers but beating them so badly that they had to be hospitalized themselves before they could be arraigned. Sally impishly kept the incident on the front pages for some days by confiding to reporters that Professor Gottesman was a practitioner of a long-forgotten martial-arts discipline, practiced only in ancient Sumer and Babylonia. "Plain childishness," she said apologetically, after the fuss had died down. "Pure self-indulgence. I'm sorry, Gus."

"Do not be," the Professor replied. "If we were to tell them the truth, I would immediately be placed in an institution." He looked sideways at his friend, who smiled and said, "What, about the rhinoceros rescuing you? I'll never tell, I swear. They could pull out my fingernails."

Professor Gottesman said, "Sally, those boys had been *trampled*, practically stamped flat. One of them had been *gored*, I saw him. Do you really think I could have done all that?"

"Remember, I've seen you in your wrath," Sally answered lightly and untruthfully. What she had in fact seen was one of the ace-of-clubs footprints she remembered in crusted mud on the Professor's front steps long ago. She said, "Gus. How old am I?"

The Professor's response was off by a number of years, as it always was. Sally said, "You've frozen me at a certain age, because you don't want me getting any older. Fine, I happen to be the same way about that rhinoceros of yours. There are one or two things I just don't want to know about that damn rhinoceros, Gus. If that's all right with you."

"Yes, Sally," Professor Gottesman answered. "That is all right."

The rhinoceros itself had very little to say about the whole incident. "I chanced to be awake, watching a lecture about Bulgarian icons on the Learning Channel. I heard the noise outside." Beyond that, it sidestepped all questions, pointedly concerning itself only with the Professor's recuperation from his injuries and shock. In fact, he recovered much faster than might reasonably have been expected from a gentleman of his years. The doctor commented on it.

The occurrence made Professor Gottesman even more of an icon himself on campus; as a direct consequence, he spent even less time there than before, except when the rhinoceros requested a particular book. Nathalie, writing from Zurich, never stopped urging him to take in a housemate, for company and safety, but she would have been utterly dumbfounded if he had accepted her suggestion. "Something looks out for him," she said to her husband. "I always knew that, I couldn't tell you why. Uncle Gustave is *somebody's* dear stuffed Charles."

Sally Lowry did grow old, despite Professor Gottesman's best efforts. The university gave her a retirement ceremony too, but she never showed up for it. "Too damn depressing," she told Professor Gottesman, as he helped her into her coat for their regular Wednesday walk "It's all right for you, Gus, you'll be around forever. Me, I drink, I still smoke, I still eat all kinds of stuff they tell me not to eat — I don't even floss, for God's sake. My circulation works like the post office, and even my cholesterol has arthritis. Only reason I've lasted this long is I had this stupid job teaching beautiful, useless stuff to idiots. Now that's it. Now I'm a goner."

"Nonsense, nonsense, Sally," Professor Gottesman assured her vigorously. "You have always told me you are too mean and spiteful to die. I am holding you to this."

"Pickled in vinegar only lasts just so long," Sally said. "One cheery note, anyway — it'll be the heart that goes. Always is, in my family. That's good, I couldn't hack cancer. I'd be a shameless, screaming disgrace, absolutely no dignity at all. I'm really grateful it'll be the heart."

The Professor was very quiet while they walked all the way down to the little local park, and back again. They had reached the apartment complex where she lived, when he suddenly gripped her by the arms, looked straight into her face, and said loudly, "That is the best heart I ever knew, yours. I will not *let* anything happen to that heart."

"Go home, Gus," Sally told him harshly. "Get out of here, go home. Christ, the only sentimental Switzer in the whole world, and I get him. Wouldn't you just know?"

Professor Gottesman actually awoke just before the telephone call came, as sometimes happens. He had dozed off in his favorite chair during a minor intellectual skirmish with the rhinoceros over Spinoza's ethics. The rhinoceros itself was sprawled in its accustomed spot, snoring authoritatively, and the kitchen clock was still striking three when the phone rang. He picked it up slowly. Sally's barely audible voice whispered, "Gus. The heart. Told you." He heard the receiver fall from her hand.

Professor Gottesman had no memory of stumbling coatless out of the house, let alone finding his car parked on the street — he was just suddenly standing by it, his hands trembling so badly as he tried to unlock the door that he dropped his keys into the gutter. How long his frantic fumbling in the darkness went on, he could never say; but at some point he became aware of a deeper darkness over him, and looked up on hands and knees to see the rhinoceros.

"On my back," it said, and no more. The Professor had barely scrambled up its warty, unyielding flanks and heaved himself precariously over the spine his legs could not straddle when there came a surge like the sea under him as the great beast leaped forward. He cried out in terror.

He would have expected, had he had wit enough at the moment to expect anything, that the rhinoceros would move at a ponderous trot, farting and rumbling, gradually building up a certain clumsy momentum. Instead, he felt himself flying, truly flying, as children know flying, flowing with the night sky, melting into the jeweled wind. If the rhinoceros's huge, flat, three-toed feet touched the ground, he never felt it: nothing existed, or ever had existed, but the sky that he was and the bodiless power that he had become — he himself, the once and foolish old Professor Gustave Gottesman, his eyes full of the light of lost stars. He even forgot Sally Lowry, only for a moment, only for the least little time.

Then he was standing in the courtyard before her house, shouting and banging maniacally on the door, pressing every button under his hand. The rhinoceros was nowhere to be seen. The building door finally buzzed open, and the Professor leaped up the stairs like a young man, calling Sally's name. Her own door was unlocked; she often left it so absentmindedly, no matter how much he scolded her about it. She was in her bedroom, half-wedged between the side of the bed and the night table, with the telephone receiver dangling by her head. Professor Gottesman touched her cheek and felt the fading warmth.

"Ah, Sally," he said. "Sally, my dear." She was very heavy, but somehow it was easy for him to lift her back onto the bed and make a place for her among the books and papers that littered the quilt, as always. He found her harmonica on the floor, and closed her fingers around it. When there was nothing more for him to do, he sat beside her, still holding her hand, until the room began to grow light. At last he said aloud, "No, the sentimental Switzer will not cry, my dear Sally," and picked up the telephone.

The rhinoceros did not return for many days after Sally Lowry's death. Professor Gottesman missed it greatly when he thought about it at all, but it was a strange, confused time. He stayed at home, hardly eating, sleeping on his feet, opening books and closing them. He never answered the telephone, and he never changed his clothes. Sometimes he wandered endlessly upstairs and down through every room in his house; sometimes he stood in one place for an hour or more at a time, staring at nothing. Occasionally the doorbell rang, and worried voices outside called his name. It was late autumn, and then winter, and the house grew cold at night, because he had forgotten to turn on the furnace. Professor Gottesman was perfectly aware of this, and other things, somewhere.

One evening, or perhaps it was early one morning, he heard the sound of water running in the bathtub upstairs. He remembered the sound, and presently he moved to his living room chair to listen to it better. For the first time in some while, he fell asleep, and woke only when he felt the rhinoceros standing over him. In the darkness he saw it only as a huge, still shadow, but it smelled unmistakably like a rhinoceros that has just had a bath. The Professor said quietly, "I wondered where you had gone."

"We unicorns mourn alone," the rhinoceros replied. "I thought it might be the same for you."

"Ah," Professor Gottesman said. "Yes, most considerate. Thank you."

He said nothing further, but sat staring into the shadow until it appeared to fold gently around him. The rhinoceros said, "We were speaking of Spinoza."

Professor Gottesman did not answer. The rhinoceros went on, "I was very interested in the comparison you drew between Spinoza and Thomas Hobbes. I would enjoy continuing our discussion."

"I do not think I can," the Professor said at last. "I do not think I want to talk anymore."

It seemed to him that the rhinoceros's eyes had become larger and brighter in its own shadow, and its horn a trifle less hulking. But its stomach rumbled as majestically as ever as it said, "In that case, perhaps we should be on our way."

"Where are we going?" Professor Gottesman asked. He was feeling oddly peaceful and disinclined to leave his chair. The rhinoceros moved closer, and for the first time that the Professor could remember its huge, hairy muzzle touched his shoulder, light as a butterfly.

"I have lived in your house for a long time," it said. "We have talked together, days and nights on end, about ways of being in this world, ways of considering it, ways of imagining it as a part of some greater imagining. Now has come the time for silence. Now I think you should come and live with me."

They were outside, on the sidewalk, in the night. Professor Gottesman had forgotten to take his coat, but he was not at all cold. He turned to look back at his house, watching it recede, its lights still burning, like a ship leaving him at his destination. He said to the rhinoceros, "What is your house like?"

"Comfortable," the rhinoceros answered. "In honesty, I would not call the hot water as superbly lavish as yours, but there is rather more room to maneuver. Especially on the stairs."

"You are walking a bit too rapidly for me," said the Professor. "May I climb on your back once more?" The rhinoceros halted immediately, saying, "By all means, please do excuse me." Professor Gottesman found it notably easier to mount this time, the massive sides having plainly grown somewhat trimmer and smoother during the rhinoceros's absence, and easier to grip with his legs. It started on briskly when he was properly settled, though not at the rapturous pace that had once married the Professor to the night wind. For some while he could hear the clopping of cloven hooves far below him, but then they seemed to fade away. He leaned forward and said into the rhinoceros's pointed silken ear, "I should tell you that I have long since come to the conclusion that you are not after all an Indian rhinoceros, but a hitherto unknown species, somehow misclassified. I hope this will not make a difference in our relationship."

"No difference, good Professor," came the gently laughing answer all around him. "No difference in the world."

COME LADY DEATH

This all happened in England a long time ago, when that George who spoke English with a heavy German accent and hated his sons was King. At that time there lived in London a lady who had nothing to do but give parties. Her name was Flora, Lady Neville, and she was a widow and very old. She lived in a great house not far from Buckingham Palace, and she had so many servants that she could not possibly remember all their names; indeed, there were some she had never even seen. She had more food than she could eat, more gowns than she could ever wear; she had wine in her cellars that no one would drink in her lifetime, and her private vaults were filled with great works of art that she did not know she owned. She spent the last years of her life giving parties and balls to which the greatest lords of England — and sometimes the King himself — came, and she was known as the wisest and wittiest woman in all London.

But in time her own parties began to bore her, and though she invited the most famous people in the land and hired the greatest jugglers and acrobats and dancers and magicians to entertain them, still she found her parties duller and duller. Listening to court gossip, which she had always loved, made her yawn. The most marvelous music, the most exciting feats of magic put her to sleep. Watching a beautiful young couple dance by her made her feel sad, and she hated to feel sad.

And so, one summer afternoon she called her closest friends around her and said to them, "More and more I find that my parties entertain everyone but me. The secret of my long life is that nothing has ever been dull for me. For all my life, I have been interested in everything I saw and been anxious to see more. But I cannot stand to be bored, and I will not go to parties at which I expect to be bored, especially if they are my own. Therefore, to my next ball I shall invite the one guest I am sure no one, not even myself, could possibly find boring. My friends, the guest of honor at my next party shall be Death himself!"

A young poet thought that this was a wonderful idea, but the rest of her friends were terrified and drew back from her. They did not want to die, they pleaded with her. Death would come for them when he was ready; why should she invite him before the appointed hour, which would arrive soon enough? But Lady Neville said, "Precisely. If Death has planned to take any of us on the night of my party, he will come whether he is invited or not. But if none of us are to die, then I think it would be charming to have Death among us — perhaps even to perform some little trick if he is in a good humor. And think of being able to say that we had been to a party with Death! All of London will envy us, all of England."

The idea began to please her friends, but a young lord, very new to London, suggested timidly, "Death is so busy. Suppose he has work to do and cannot accept your invitation?"

"No one has ever refused an invitation of mine," said Lady Neville, "not even the King." And the young lord was not invited to her party.

She sat down then and there and wrote out the invitation. There was some dispute among her friends as to how they should address Death. "His Lordship Death" seemed to place him only on the level of a viscount or a baron. "His Grace Death" met with more acceptance, but Lady Neville said it sounded hypocritical. And to refer to Death as "His Majesty" was to make him the equal of the King of England, which even Lady Neville would not dare to do. It was finally decided that all should speak of him as "His Eminence Death," which pleased nearly everyone.

Captain Compson, known both as England's most dashing cavalry officer and most elegant rake, remarked next, "That's all very well, but how is the invitation to reach Death? Does anyone here know where he lives?"

"Death undoubtedly lives in London," said Lady Neville, "like everyone else of any importance, though he probably goes to Deauville for the summer. Actually, Death must live fairly near my own house. This is much the best section of London, and you could hardly expect a person of Death's importance to live anywhere else. When I stop to think of it, it's really rather strange that we haven't met before now, on the street."

Most of her friends agreed with her, but the poet, whose name was David Lorimond, cried out, "No, my lady, you are wrong! Death lives among the poor. Death lives in the foulest, darkest alleys of this city, in some vile, rat-ridden hovel that smells of —" He stopped here, partly because Lady Neville had indicated her displeasure, and partly because he had never been inside such a hut or thought of wondering what it smelled like. "Death lives among the poor," he went on, "and comes to visit them every day, for he is their only friend."

Lady Neville answered him as coldly as she had spoken to the young lord. "He may be forced to deal with them, David, but I hardly think that he seeks them out as companions. I am certain that it is as difficult for him to think of the poor as individuals as it is for me. Death is, after all, a nobleman."

There was no real argument among the lords and ladies that Death lived in a neighborhood at least as good as their own, but none of them seemed to know the name of Death's street, and no one had ever seen Death's house.

"If there were a war," Captain Compson said, "Death would be easy to find. I have seen him, you know, even spoken to him, but he has never answered me."

"Quite proper," said Lady Neville. "Death must always speak first. You are not a very correct person, Captain," but she smiled at him, as all women did.

Then an idea came to her. "My hairdresser has a sick child, I understand," she said. "He was telling me about it yesterday, sounding most dull and hopeless. I will send for him and give him the invitation, and he in his turn can give it to Death when he comes to take the brat. A bit unconventional, I admit, but I see no other way."

"If he refuses?" asked a lord who had just been married. "Why should he?" asked Lady Neville.

Again it was the poet who exclaimed amidst the general approval that it was a cruel and wicked thing to do. But he fell silent when Lady Neville innocently asked him, "Why, David?"

So the hairdresser was sent for, and when he stood before them, smiling nervously and twisting his hands to be in the same room with so many great lords, Lady Neville told him the errand that was required of him. And she was right, as she usually was, for he made no refusal. He merely took the invitation in his hand and asked to be excused.

He did not return for two days, but when he did he presented himself to Lady Neville without being sent for and handed her a small white envelope. Saying, "How very nice of you, thank you very much," she opened it and found therein a plain calling card with nothing on it except these words:

*Death will be pleased to attend
Lady Neville's ball.*

"Death gave you this?" she asked the hairdresser eagerly. "What was he like?" But the hairdresser stood still, looking past her, and said nothing, and she, not really waiting for an answer, called a dozen servants to her and told them to run and summon her friends. As she paced up and down the room waiting for them, she asked again, "What is Death like?" The hairdresser did not reply.

When her friends came they passed the little card excitedly from hand to hand, until it had gotten quite smudged and bent from their fingers. But they all admitted that, beyond its message, there was nothing particularly unusual about it. It was neither hot nor cold to the touch, and what little odor clung to it was rather pleasant. Everyone said that it was a very familiar smell, but no one could give it a name. The poet said that it reminded him of lilacs but not exactly.

It was Captain Compson, however, who pointed out the one thing that no one else had noticed. "Look at the handwriting itself," he said. "Have you ever seen anything more graceful? The letters seem as light as birds. I think we have wasted our time speaking of Death as His This and His That. A woman wrote this note."

Then there was an uproar and a great babble, and the card had to be handed around again so that everyone could exclaim, "Yes, by God!" over it. The voice of the poet rose out the hubbub saying, "It is very natural, when you come to think of it. After all, the French say *la mort.* Lady Death. I should much prefer Death to be a woman."

"Death rides a great black horse," said Captain Compson firmly, "and wears armor of the same color. Death is very tall, taller than anyone. It was no woman I saw on the battlefield, striking right and left like any soldier. Perhaps the hairdresser wrote it himself, or the hairdresser's wife." But the hairdresser refused to speak, though they gathered around him and begged him to say who had given him the note. At first they promised him all sorts of rewards, and later they threatened to do terrible things to him. "Did you write this card?" he was asked, and "Who wrote it, then? Was it a living woman? Was it really Death? Did Death say anything to you? How did you know it was Death? Is Death a woman? Are you trying to make fools of us all?"

Not a word from the hairdresser, not one word, and finally Lady Neville called her servants to have him whipped and thrown into the street. He did not look at her as they took him away, or utter a sound.

Silencing her friends with a wave of her hand, Lady Neville said, "The ball will take place two weeks from tonight. Let Death come as Death pleases, whether as a man or woman or strange, sexless creature." She smiled calmly. "Death may well be a woman," she said. "I am less certain of Death's form than I was, but I am also less frightened of Death. I am too old to be afraid of anything that can use a quill pen to write me a letter. Go home now, and as you make your preparations for the ball see that you speak of it to your servants, that they may spread the news all over London. Let it be known that on this one night no one in the world will die, for Death will be dancing at Lady Neville's ball."

For the next two weeks Lady Neville's great house shook and groaned and creaked like an old tree in a gale as the servants hammered and scrubbed, polished and painted, making ready for the ball. Lady Neville had always been very proud of her house, but as the ball drew near she began to be afraid that it would not be nearly grand enough for Death, who was surely accustomed to visiting in the homes of richer, mightier people than herself. Fearing the scorn of Death, she worked night and day supervising her servants' preparations. Curtains and carpets had to be cleaned, goldwork and silverware polished until they gleamed by themselves in the dark. The grand staircase that rushed down into the ballroom like a waterfall was washed and rubbed so often that it was almost impossible to walk on it without slipping. As for the ballroom itself, it took thirty-two servants working at once to clean it properly, not counting those who were polishing the glass chandelier that was taller than a man and the fourteen smaller lamps. And when they were done she made them do it all over, not because she saw any dust or dirt anywhere, but because she was sure that Death would.

As for herself, she chose her finest gown and saw to the laundering personally. She called in another hairdresser and had him put up her hair in the style of an earlier time, wanting to show Death that she was a woman who enjoyed her age and did not find it necessary to ape the young and beautiful. All the day of the ball she sat before her mirror, not making herself up much beyond the normal touches of rouge and eye shadow and fine rice powder, but staring at the lean old face she had been born with, wondering how it would appear to Death. Her steward asked her to approve his wine selection, but she sent him away and stayed at her mirror until it was time to dress and go downstairs to meet her guests.

Everyone arrived early. When she looked out of a window, Lady Neville saw that the driveway of her home was choked with carriages and fine horses. "It all looks like a funeral procession," she said. The footman cried the names of her guests to the echoing ballroom. "Captain Henry Compson, His Majesty's Household Cavalry! Mr. David Lorimond! Lord and Lady Torrance!!" (They were the youngest couple there, having been married only three months before.) "Sir Roger Harbison! The Contessa della Candini!" Lady Neville permitted them all to kiss her hand and made them welcome.

She had engaged the finest musicians she could find to play for the dancing, but though they began to play at her signal, not one couple stepped out on the floor, nor did one young lord approach her to request the honor of the first dance, as was proper. They milled together, shining and murmuring, their eyes fixed on the ballroom door. Every time they heard a carriage clatter up the driveway they seemed to flinch a little and draw closer together; every time the footman announced the arrival of another guest, they all sighed softly and swayed a little on their feet with relief.

"Why did they come to my party if they were afraid?" Lady Neville muttered scornfully to herself. "I am not afraid of meeting Death. I ask only that Death may be impressed by the magnificence of my house and the flavor of my wines. I will die sooner than anyone here, but I am not afraid." Certain that Death would not arrive until midnight, she moved among her guests, attempting to calm them, not with her words, which she knew they would not hear, but with the tone of her voice as if they were so many frightened horses. But little by little, she herself was infected by their nervousness: whenever she sat down she stood up again immediately, she tasted a dozen glasses of wine without finishing any of them, and she glanced constantly at her jeweled watch, at first wanting to hurry the midnight along and end the waiting, later scratching at the watch face with her forefinger, as if she would push away the night and drag the sun backward into the sky. When midnight came, she was standing with the rest of them, breathing through her mouth, shifting from foot to foot, listening for the sound of carriage wheels turning in gravel.

When the clock began to strike midnight, everyone, even Lady Neville and the brave Captain Compson, gave one startled little cry and then was silent again, listening to the tolling of the clock. The smaller clocks upstairs began to chime. Lady Neville's ears hurt. She caught sight of herself in the ballroom mirror, one gray face turned up toward the ceiling as if she were gasping for air, and she thought, "Death will be a woman, a hideous, filthy old crone as tall and strong as a man. And the most terrible thing of all will be that she will have my face." All the clocks stopped striking, and Lady Neville closed her eyes.

She opened them again only when she heard the whispering around her take on a different tone, one in which fear was fused with relief and a certain chagrin. For no new carriage stood in the driveway. Death had not come. The noise grew slowly louder; here and there people were beginning to laugh. Near her, Lady Neville heard young Lord Torrance say to his wife, "There, my darling, I told you there was nothing to be afraid of. It was all a joke."

"I am ruined," Lady Neville thought. The laughter was increasing; it pounded against her ears in strokes, like the chiming of the clocks. "I wanted to give a ball so grand that those who were not invited would be shamed in front of the whole city, and this is my reward. I am ruined, and I deserve it."

Turning to the poet Lorimond, she said, "Dance with me, David." She signaled to the musicians, who at once began to play. When Lorimond hesitated, she said, "Dance with me now. You will not have another chance. I shall never give a party again."

Lorimond bowed and led her onto the dance floor. The guests parted for them, and the laughter died down for a moment, but Lady Neville knew that it would soon begin again. "Well, let them laugh," she thought. "I did not fear Death when they were all trembling. Why should I fear their laughter?" But she could feel a stinging at the thin lids of her eyes, and she closed them once more as she began to dance with Lorimond.

And then, quite suddenly, all the carriage horses outside the house whinnied loudly, just once, as the guests had cried out at midnight. There were a great many horses, and their one salute was so loud that everyone in the room became instantly silent. They heard the heavy steps of the footman as he went to open the door, and they shivered as if they felt the cool breeze that drifted into the house. Then they heard a light voice saying, "Am I late? Oh, I am so sorry. The horses were tired," and before the footman could re-enter to announce her, a lovely young girl in a white dress stepped gracefully into the ballroom doorway and stood there smiling.

She could not have been more than nineteen. Her hair was yellow, and she wore it long. It fell thickly upon her bare shoulders that gleamed warmly through it, two limestone islands rising out of a dark golden sea. Her face was wide at the forehead and cheekbones, and narrow at the chin, and her skin was so clear that many of the ladies there — Lady Neville among them — touched their own faces wonderingly, and instantly drew their hands away as though their own skin had rasped their fingers. Her mouth was pale, where the mouths of other women were red and orange and even purple. Her eyebrows, thicker and straighter than was fashionable, met over dark, calm eyes that were set so deep in her young face and were so black, so uncompromisingly black, that the middle-aged wife of a middle-aged lord murmured, "Touch of a gypsy there, I think."

"Or something worse," suggested her husband's mistress. "Be silent!" Lady Neville spoke louder than she had intended, and the girl turned to look at her. She smiled, and Lady Neville tried to smile back, but her mouth seemed very stiff. "Welcome," she said. "Welcome, my lady Death."

A sigh rustled among the lords and ladies as the girl took the old woman's hand and curtsied to her, sinking and rising in one motion, like a wave. "You are Lady Neville," she said. "Thank you so much for inviting me." Her accent was as faint and almost familiar as her perfume.

"Please excuse me for being late," she said earnestly. "I had to come from a long way off, and my horses are so tired."

"The groom will rub them down," Lady Neville said, "and feed them if you wish."

"Oh, no," the girl answered quickly. "Tell him not to go near the horses, please. They are not really horses, and they are very fierce."

She accepted a glass of wine from a servant and drank it slowly, sighing softly and contentedly. "What good wine," she said. "And what a beautiful house you have."

"Thank you," said Lady Neville. Without turning, she could feel every woman in the room envying her, sensing it as she could always sense the approach of rain.

"I wish I lived here," Death said in her low, sweet voice. "I will, one day."

Then, seeing Lady Neville become as still as if she had turned to ice, she put her hand on the old woman's arm and said, "Oh, I'm sorry, I'm so sorry. I am so cruel, but I never mean to be. Please forgive me, Lady Neville. I am not used to company, and I do such stupid things. Please forgive me." Her hand felt as light and warm on Lady Neville's arm as the hand of any other young girl, and her eyes were so appealing that Lady Neville replied, "You have said nothing wrong. While you are my guest, my house is yours."

"Thank you," said Death, and she smile so radiantly that the musicians began to play quite by themselves, and with no sign from Lady Neville. She would have stopped them, but Death said, "Oh, what lovely music! Let them play, please."

So the musicians played a gavotte, and Death, unabashed by eyes that stared at her in greedy terror, sang softly to herself without words, lifted her white gown slightly with both hands, and made hesitant little patting steps with her small feet. "I have not danced in so long," she said wistfully. "I'm quite sure I've forgotten how."

She was shy; she would not look up to embarrass the young lords, not one of whom stepped forward to dance with her. Lady Neville felt a flood of shame and sympathy, emotions she thought had withered in her years ago. "Is she to be humiliated at my own ball?" she thought angrily. "It is because she is Death; if she were the ugliest, foulest hag in all the world they would clamor to dance with her, because they are gentlemen and they know what is expected of them. But no gentleman will dance with Death, no matter how beautiful she is." She glance sideways at David Lorimond. His face was flushed, and his hands were clasped so tightly as he stared at Death that his fingers were like glass, but when Lady Neville touched his arm he did not turn, and when she hissed, "David!", he pretended not to hear her.

Then Captain Compson, gray-haired and handsome in his uniform, stepped out of the crowd and bowed gracefully before Death. "If I may have the honor," he said.

"Captain Compson," said Death, smiling. She put her arm in his. "I was hoping you would ask me."

This brought a frown from the older women, who did not consider it a proper thing to say, but for that Death cared not a rap. Captain Compson led her to the center of the floor, and there they danced. Death was curiously graceless at first — she was too anxious to please her partner, and she seemed to have no notion of rhythm. The Captain himself moved with the mixture of dignity and humor that Lady Neville had never seen in another man, but when he looked at her over Death's shoulder, she saw something that no one else appeared to notice: that his face and eyes were immobile with fear, and that, though he offered Death his hand with easy gallantry, he flinched slightly when she took it. And yet he danced as well as Lady Neville had ever seen him.

"Ah, that's what comes of having a reputation to maintain," she thought. "Captain Compson too must do what is expected of him. I hope someone else will dance with her soon."

But no one did. Little by little, other couples overcame their fear and slipped hurriedly out on the floor when Death was looking the other way, but nobody sought to relieve Captain Compson of his beautiful partner. They danced every dance together. In time, some of the men present began to look at her with more appreciation than terror, but when she returned their glances and smiled at them, they clung to their partners as if a cold wind were threatening to blow them away.

One of the few who stared at her frankly and with pleasure was young Lord Torrance, who usually danced only with his wife. Another was the poet Lorimond. Dancing with Lady Neville, he remarked to her, "If she is Death, what do these frightened fools think they are? If she is ugliness, what must they be? I hate their fear. It is obscene."

Death and the Captain danced past them at that moment, and they heard him say to her, "But if that was truly you that I saw in the battle, how can you have changed so? How can you have become so lovely?"

Death's laughter was gay and soft. "I thought that among so many beautiful people it might be better to be beautiful. I was afraid of frightening everyone and spoiling the party."

"They all thought she would be ugly," said Lorimond to Lady Neville. "I — I knew she would be beautiful."

"Then why have you not danced with her?" Lady Neville asked him. "Are you also afraid?"

"No, oh, no," the poet answered quickly and passionately. "I will ask her to dance very soon. I only want to look at her a little longer."

The musicians played on and on. The dancing wore away the night as slowly as falling water wears down a cliff. It seemed to Lady Neville that no night had ever endured longer, and yet she was neither tired nor bored. She danced with every man there, except with Lord Torrance, who was dancing with his wife as if they had just met that night, and, of course, with Captain Compson. Once he lifted his hand and touched Death's golden hair very lightly. He was a striking man still, a fit partner for so beautiful a girl, but Lady Neville looked at his face each time she passed him and realized that he was older than anyone knew.

Death herself seemed younger than the youngest there. No woman at the ball danced better than she now, though it was hard for Lady Neville to remember at what point her awkwardness had given way to the liquid sweetness of her movements. She smiled and called to everyone who caught her eye — and she knew them all by name; she sang constantly, making up words to the dance tunes, nonsense words, sounds without meaning, and yet everyone strained to hear her soft voice without knowing why. And when, during a waltz, she caught up the trailing end of her gown to give her more freedom as she danced, she seemed to Lady Neville to move like a little sailing boat over a still evening sea.

Lady Neville heard Lady Torrance arguing angrily with the Contessa della Candini. "I don't care if she is Death, she's no older than I am, she can't be!"

"Nonsense," said the Contessa, who could not afford to be generous to any other woman. "She is twenty-eight, thirty, if she is an hour. And that dress, that bridal gown she wears — really!"

"Vile," said the woman who had come to the ball as Captain Compson's freely acknowledged mistress. "Tasteless. But one should know better than to expect taste from Death, I suppose." Lady Torrance looked as if she were going to cry.

"They are jealous of Death," Lady Neville said to herself. "How strange. I am not jealous of her, not in the least. And I do not fear her at all." She was very proud of herself.

Then, as unbiddenly as they had begun to play, the musicians stopped. They began to put away their instruments. In the sudden shrill silence, Death pulled away from Captain Compson and ran to look out of one of the tall windows, pushing the curtains apart with both hands.

"Look!" she said, with her back turned to them. "Come and look. The night is almost gone."

The summer sky was still dark, and the eastern horizon was only a shade lighter than the rest of the sky, but the stars had vanished and the trees near the house were gradually becoming distinct. Death pressed her face against the window and said, so softly that the other guests could barely hear her, "I must go now."

"No," Lady Neville said, and was not immediately aware that she had spoken. "You must stay a while longer. The ball was in your honor. Please stay."

Death held out both hands to her, and Lady Neville came and took them in her own. "I've had a wonderful time," she said gently. "You cannot possibly imagine how it feels to be actually invited to such a ball as this, because you have given them and gone to them all your life. One is like another to you, but for me it is different. Do you understand me?" Lady Neville nodded silently. "I will remember this night forever," Death said.

"Stay," Captain Compson said. "Stay just a little longer." He put his hand on Death's shoulder, and she smiled and leaned her cheek against it. "Dear Captain Compson," she said. "My first real gallant. Aren't you tired of me yet?"

"Never," he said. "Please stay."

"Stay," said Lorimond, and he too seemed about to touch her. "Stay. I want to talk to you. I want to look at you. I will dance with you if you stay."

"How many followers I have," Death said in wonder. She stretched her hand toward Lorimond, but he drew back from her and then flushed in shame. "A soldier and a poet. How wonderful it is to be a woman. But why did you not speak to me earlier, both of you? Now it is too late. I must go."

"Please, stay," Lady Torrance whispered. She held on to her husband's hand for courage. "We think you are so beautiful, both of us do."

"Gracious Lady Torrance," the girl said kindly. She turned back to the window, touched it lightly, and it flew open. The cool dawn air rushed into the ballroom, fresh with rain but already smelling faintly of the London streets over which it had passed. They heard birdsong and the strange, harsh nickering of Death's horses.

"Do you want me to stay?" she asked. The question was put, not to Lady Neville, nor to Captain Compson, nor to any of her admirers, but to the Contessa della Candini, who stood well back from them all, hugging her flowers to herself and humming a little song of irritation. She did not in the least want Death to stay, but she was afraid that all the other women would think her envious of Death's beauty, and so she said, "Yes. Of course I do."

"Ah," said Death. She was almost whispering. "And you," she said to another woman, "do you want me to stay? Do you want me to be one of your friends?"

"Yes," said the woman, "because you are beautiful and a true lady."

"And you," said Death to a man, "and you," to a woman, "and you," to another man, "do you want me to stay?" And they all answered, "Yes, Lady Death, we do."

"Do you want me, then?" she cried at last to all them. "Do you want me to live among you and to be one of you, and not to be Death anymore? Do you want me to visit your houses and come to all your parties? Do you want me to ride horses like yours instead of mine, do you want me to wear the kind of dresses you wear, and say the things you would say? Would one of you marry me, and would the rest of you dance at my wedding and bring gifts to my children? Is that what you want?"

"Yes," said Lady Neville. "Stay here, stay with me, stay with us."

Death's voice, without becoming louder, had become clearer and older; too old a voice, thought Lady Neville, for such a young girl. "Be sure," said Death. "Be sure of what you want, be very sure. Do all of you want me to stay? For if one of you says to me, no, go away, then I must leave at once and never return. Be sure. Do you all want me?"

And everyone there cried with one voice, "Yes! Yes, you must stay with us. You are so beautiful that we cannot let you go."

"We are tired," said Captain Compson.

"We are blind," said Lorimond, adding, "especially to poetry."

"We are afraid," said Lord Torrance quietly, and his wife took his arm and said, "Both of us."

"We are dull and stupid," said Lady Neville, "and growing old uselessly. Stay with us, Lady Death."

And then Death smiled sweetly and radiantly and took a step forward, and it was as though she had come down among them from a very great height. "Very well," she said. "I will stay with you. I will be

Death no more. I will be a woman."

The room was full of a deep sigh, although no one was seen to open his mouth. No one moved, for the golden-haired girl was Death still, and her horses still whinnied for her outside. No one could look at her for long, although she was the most beautiful girl anyone there had ever seen. "There is a price to pay," she said. "There is always a price. Some one of you must become Death in my place, for there must forever be Death in the world. Will anyone choose? Will anyone here become Death of his own free will? For only thus can I become a human girl."

No one spoke, no one spoke at all. But they backed slowly away from her, like waves slipping back down a beach to the sea when you try to catch them. The Contessa della Candini and her friends would have crept quietly out of the door, but Death smiled at them and they stood where they were. Captain Compson opened his mouth as though he were going to declare himself, but he said nothing. Lady Neville did not move.

"No one," said Death. She touched a flower with her finger, and it seemed to crouch and flex itself like a pleased cat. "No one at all," she said. "Then I must choose, and that is just, for that is the way I became Death. I never wanted to be Death, and it makes me so happy that you want me to become one of yourselves. I have searched a long time for people who would want me. Now I have only to choose someone to replace me and it is done. I will choose very carefully."

"Oh, we were so foolish," Lady Neville said to herself. "We were so foolish." But she said nothing aloud; she merely clasped her hands and stared at the young girl, thinking vaguely that if she had had a daughter she would have been greatly pleased if she resembled the lady Death.

"The Contessa della Candini," said Death thoughtfully, and that woman gave a little squeak of terror because she could not draw her breath for a scream. But Death laughed and said, "No, that would be silly." She said nothing more, but for a long time after that the Contessa burned with humiliation at not having been chosen to be Death.

"Not Captain Compson," murmured Death, "because he is too kind to become Death, and because it would be too cruel to him. He wants to die so badly." The expression on the Captain's face did not change, but his hands began to tremble.

"Not Lorimond," the girl continued, "because he knows so little about life, and because I like him." The poet flushed, and turned white, and then turned pink again. He made as if to kneel clumsily on one knee, but instead he pulled himself erect and stood as much like Captain Compson as he could. "Not the Torrances," said Death, "never Lord and Lady Torrance, for both of them care too much about another person to take any pride in being Death." But she hesitated over Lady Torrance for a while, staring at her out of her dark and curious eyes. "I was your age when I became Death," she said at last. "I wonder what it will be like to be your age again. I have been Death for so long." Lady Torrance shivered and did not speak.

And at last Death said quietly, "Lady Neville."

"I am here," Lady Neville answered.

"I think you are the only one," said Death. "I choose you, Lady Neville."

Again Lady Neville heard every guest sigh softly, and although her back was to them all she knew that they were sighing in relief that neither themselves nor anyone dear to themselves had been chosen. Lady Torrance gave a little cry of protest, but Lady Neville knew that she would have cried out at whatever choice Death made. She heard herself say calmly, "I am honored. But was there no one more worthy than I?"

"Not one," said Death. "There is no one quite so weary of being human, no one who knows better how meaningless it is to be alive. And there is no one else here with the power to treat life" — and she smiled sweetly and cruelly — "the life of your hairdresser's child, for instance, as the meaningless thing it is. Death has a heart, but it is forever an empty heart, and I think, Lady Neville, that your heart is like a dry riverbed, like a seashell. You will be very content as Death, more so than I , for I was very young when I became Death."

She came toward Lady Neville, light and swaying, her deep eyes wide and full of the light of the red morning sun that was beginning to rise. The guests at the ball moved back from her, although she did not look at them, but Lady Neville clenched her hands tightly and watched Death come toward her with little dancing steps. "We must kiss each other," Death said. "That is the way I became Death." She shook her head delightedly, so that her soft hair swirled about her shoulders. "Quickly, quickly," she said. "Oh, I cannot wait to be human again."

"You may not like it," Lady Neville said. She felt very calm, though she could hear her old heart pounding in her chest and feel it in the tips of her fingers. "You may not like it after a while," she said.

"Perhaps not." Death's smile was very close to her now. "I will not be as beautiful as I am, and perhaps people will not love me as much as they do now. But I will be human for a while, and at last I will die. I have done my penance."

"What penance?" the old woman asked the beautiful girl. "What was it you did? Why did you become Death?"

"I don't remember," said the lady Death. "And you too will forget in time." She was smaller than Lady Neville, and so much younger. In her white dress she might have been the daughter that Lady Neville had never had, who would have been with her always and held her mother's head lightly in the crook of her arm when she felt old and sad. Now she lifted her head to kiss Lady Neville's cheek, and as she did so she whispered in her hear, "You will still be beautiful when I am ugly. Be kind to me then."

Behind Lady Neville the handsome gentlemen and ladies murmured and sighed, fluttering like moths in their evening dress, in their elegant gowns. "I promise," she said, and then she pursed her dry lips to kiss the soft, sweet-smelling cheek of the young Lady Death.

LILA THE WEREWOLF

Lila Braun had been living with Farrell for three weeks before he found out she was a werewolf. They had met at a party when the moon was a few nights past the full, and by the time it had withered to the shape of a lemon Lila had moved her suitcase, her guitar, and her Ewan MacColl records two blocks north and four blocks west to Farrell's apartment on Ninety-eighth Street. Girls sometimes happened to Farrell like that.

One evening, Lila wasn't in when Farrell came home from work at the bookstore. She had left a note on the table, under a can of tuna fish. The note said that she had gone up to the Bronx to have dinner with her mother, and would probably be spending the night there. The coleslaw in the refrigerator should be finished before it went bad.

Farrell ate the tuna fish and gave the coleslaw to Grunewald. Grunewald was a half-grown Russian wolfhound, the color of sour milk. He looked like a goat, and had no outside interests except shoes. Farrell was taking care of him for a girl who was away in Europe for the summer. She sent Grunewald a tape recording of her voice every week.

Farrell went to a movie with a friend, and to the West End afterward for beer. Then he walked home alone under the full moon, which was red and yellow. He reheated the morning coffee, played a record, read through a week-old 'News Of The Week In Review' section of the Sunday *Times*, and finally took Grunewald up to the roof for the night, as he always did. The dog had been accustomed to sleep in the same bed with his mistress, and the point was not negotiable. Grunewald mooed and scrabbled and butted all the way, but Farrell pushed him out among the looming chimneys and ventilators and slammed the door. Then he came back downstairs and went to bed.

He slept very badly. Grunewald's baying woke him twice; and there was something else that brought him half out of bed, thirsty and lonely, with his sinuses full and the night swaying like a curtain as the figures of his dream scurried offstage. Grunewald seemed to have gone off the air — perhaps it was the silence that had awakened him. Whatever the reason, he never really got back to sleep.

He was lying on his back, watching a chair with his clothes on it becoming a chair again, when the wolf came in through the open window. It landed lightly in the middle of the room and stood there for a moment, breathing quickly, with its ears back. There was blood on the wolf's teeth and tongue, and blood on its chest.

Farrell, whose true gift was for acceptance, especially in the morning, accepted the idea that there was a wolf in his bedroom and lay quite still, closing his eyes as the grim, black-lipped head swung towards him. Having once worked at a zoo, he was able to recognize the beast as a Central European subspecies: smaller and lighter-boned than the northern timber wolf variety, lacking the thick, ruffy mane at the shoulders and having a more pointed nose and ears. His own pedantry always delighted him, even at the worst moments.

Blunt claws clicking on the linoleum, then silent on the throw rug by the bed. Something warm and slow splashed down on his shoulder, but he never moved. The wild smell of the wolf was over him, and that did frighten him at last to be in the same room with that smell and the Miro prints on the walls. Then he felt the sunlight on his eyelids, and at the same moment he heard the wolf moan softly and deeply.

The sound was not repeated, but the breath on his face was suddenly sweet and smoky, dizzyingly familiar after the other. He opened his eyes and saw Lila. She was sitting naked on the edge of the bed, smiling, with her hair down.

"Hello, baby," she said. "Move over, baby. I came home."

Farrell's gift was for acceptance. He was perfectly willing to believe that he had dreamed the wolf; to believe Lila's story of boiled chicken and bitter arguments and sleeplessness on Tremont Avenue; and to forget that her first caress had been to bite him on the shoulder, hard enough so that the blood crusting there as he got up and made breakfast might very well be his own. But then he left the coffee perking and went up to the roof to get Grunewald. He found the dog sprawled in a grove of TV antennas, looking more like a goat than ever, with his throat torn out. Farrell had never actually seen an animal with its throat torn out.

The coffeepot was still chuckling when he came back into the apartment, which struck him as very odd. You could have either werewolves or Pyrex nine-cup percolators in the world, but not both, surely. He told Lila, watching her face. She was a small girl, not really pretty, but with good eyes and a lovely mouth, and with a curious sullen gracefulness that had been the first thing to speak to Farrell at the party. When he told her how Grunewald had looked, she shivered all over, once.

"Ugh!" she said, wrinkling her lips back from her neat white teeth. "Oh baby, how awful. Poor Grunewald. Oh, poor Barbara." Barbara was Grunewald's owner.

"Yeah," Farrell said. "Poor Barbara, making her little tapes in Saint-Tropez." He could not look away from Lila's face.

She said, "Wild dogs. Not really wild, I mean, but with owners. You hear about it sometimes, how a pack of them get together and attack children and things, running through the streets. Then they go home and eat their Dog Yummies. The scary thing is that they probably live right around here. Everybody on the block seems to have a dog. God, that's scary. Poor Grunewald."

"They didn't tear him up much," Farrell said. "It must have been just for the fun of it. And the blood. I didn't know dogs killed for the blood. He didn't have any blood left."

The tip of Lila's tongue appeared between her lips, in the unknowing reflex of a fondled cat. As evidence, it wouldn't have stood up even in old Salem; but Farrell knew the truth then, beyond laziness or rationalization, and went on buttering toast for Lila. Farrell had nothing against werewolves, and he had never liked Grunewald.

He told his friend Ben Kassoy about Lila when they met in the Automat for lunch. He had to shout it over the clicking and rattling all around them, but the people sitting six inches away on either hand never looked up. New Yorkers never eavesdrop. They hear only what they simply cannot help hearing.

Ben said, "I told you about Bronx girls. You better come stay at my place for a few days."

Farrell shook his head. "No, that's silly. I mean, it's only Lila. If she were going to hurt me, she could have done it last night. Besides, it won't happen again for a month. There has to be a full moon."

His friend stared at him. "So what? What's that got to do with anything? You going to go on home as though nothing had happened?"

"Not as though nothing had happened," Farrell said lamely. "The thing is, it's still only Lila, not Lon Chaney or somebody. Look, she goes to her psychiatrist three afternoons a week, and she's got her guitar lesson one night a week, and her pottery class one night, and she cooks eggplant maybe twice a week. She calls her mother every Friday night, and one night a month she turns into a wolf. You see what I'm getting at? It's still Lila, whatever she does, and I just can't get terribly shook about it. A little bit, sure, because what the hell. But I don't know. Anyway, there's no mad rush about it. I'll talk to her when the thing comes up in conversation, just naturally. It's okay."

Ben said, "God damn. You see why nobody has any respect for liberals anymore? Farrell, I know you. You're just scared of hurting her feelings."

"Well, it's that too," Farrell agreed, a little embarrassed. "I hate confrontations. If I break up with her now, she'll think I'm doing it because she's a werewolf. It's awkward, it feels nasty and middle-class. I should have broken up with her the first time I met her mother, or the second time she served the eggplant. Her mother, boy, there's the real werewolf, there's somebody I'd wear wolfsbane against, that woman. Damn, I wish I hadn't found out. I don't think I've ever found out anything about people that I was the better for knowing."

Ben walked all the way back to the bookstore with him, arguing. It touched Farrell, because Ben hated to walk. Before they parted, Ben suggested, "At least you could try some of that stuff you were talking about, the wolfsbane. There's garlic, too — you put some in a little bag and wear it around your neck. Don't laugh, man. If there's such a thing as werewolves, the other stuff must be real, too. Cold iron, silver, oak, running water — "

"I'm not laughing at you," Farrell said, but he was still grinning. "Lila's shrink says she has a rejection thing, very deep-seated, take us years to break through all that scar tissue. Now if I start walking around wearing amulets and mumbling in Latin every time she looks at me, who knows how far it'll set her back? Listen, I've done some things I'm not proud of, but I don't want to mess with anyone's analysis. That's the sin against God." He sighed and slapped Ben lightly on the arm. "Don't worry about it. We'll work it out, I'll talk to her."

But between that night and the next full moon, he found no good, casual way of bringing the subject up. Admittedly, he did not try as hard as he might have: it was true that he feared confrontations more than he feared werewolves, and he would have found it almost as difficult to talk to Lila about her guitar playing, or her pots, or the political arguments she got into at parties. "The thing is," he said to Ben, "it's sort of one more little weakness not to take advantage of. In a way."

They made love often that month. The smell of Lila flowered in the bedroom, where the smell of the wolf still lingered almost visibly, and both of them were wild, heavy zoo smells, warm and raw and fearful, the sweeter for being savage. Farrell held Lila in his arms and knew what she was, and he was always frightened; but he would not have let her go if she had turned into a wolf again as he held her It was a relief to peer at her while she slept and see how stubby and childish her fingernails were, or that the skin around her mouth was rashy because she had been snacking on chocolate. She loved secret sweets, but they always betrayed her.

It's only Lila after all, he would think as he drowsed off. Her mother used to hide the candy, but Lila always found it. Now she's a big girl, neither married nor in graduate school, but living in sin with an Irish musician, and she can have all the candy she wants. What kind of a werewolf is that. Poor Lila, practicing *Who killed Davey Moore? Why did he die?. . .*

The note said that she would be working late at the magazine, on layout, and might have to be there all night. Farrell put on about four feet of Telemann laced with Django Reinhardt, took down *The Golden Bough*, and settled into a chair by the window. The moon shone in at him, bright and thin and sharp as the lid of a tin can, and it did not seem to move at all as he dozed and woke.

Lila's mother called several times during the night, which was interesting. Lila still picked up her mail and most messages at her old apartment, and her two roommates covered for her when necessary, but Farrell was absolutely certain that her mother knew she was living with him. Farrell was an expert on mothers. Mrs. Braun called him Joe each time she called and that made him wonder, for he knew she hated him. Does she suspect that we share a secret? Ah, poor Lila.

The last time the telephone woke him, it was still dark in the room, but the traffic lights no longer glittered through rings of mist, and the cars made a different sound on the warming pavement. A man was saying clearly in the street, "Well, I'd shoot'm. I'd shoot'm." Farrell let the telephone ring ten times before he picked it up.

"Let me talk to Lila," Mrs. Braun said.

"She isn't here." What if the sun catches her, what if she turns back to herself in front of a cop, or a bus driver, or a couple of nuns going to early Mass? "Lila isn't here, Mrs. Braun."

"I have reason to believe that's not true." The fretful, muscular voice had dropped all pretense of warmth. "I want to talk to Lila."

Farrell was suddenly dry-mouthed and shivering with fury. It was her choice of words that did it. "Well, I have reason to believe you're a suffocating old bitch and a bourgeois Stalinist. How do you like them apples, Mrs. B?" As though his anger had summoned her, the wolf was standing two feet away from him. Her coat was dark and lank with sweat, and yellow saliva was mixed with the blood that strung from her jaws. She looked at Farrell and growled far away in her throat.

"Just a minute," he said. He covered the receiver with his palm. "It's for you," he said to the wolf. "It's your mother." The wolf made a pitiful sound, almost inaudible, and scuffed at the floor. She was plainly exhausted. Mrs. Braun pinged in Farrell's ear like a bug against a lighted window. "What, what? Hello, what is this? Listen, you put Lila on the phone right now. Hello? I want to talk to Lila. I know she's there."

Farrell hung up just as the sun touched a corner of the window. The wolf became Lila. As before, she only made one sound. The phone rang again, and she picked it up without a glance at Farrell. "Bernice?" Lila always called her mother by her first name. "Yes — no, no — yeah, I'm fine. I'm all right, I just forgot to call. No, I'm all right, will you listen? Bernice, there's no law that says you have to get hysterical. Yes, you are." She dropped down on the bed, groping under her pillow for cigarettes. Farrell got up and began to make coffee.

"Well, there was a little trouble," Lila was saying. "See, I went to the zoo, because I couldn't find — Bernice, I know, I *know*, but that was, what, three months ago. The thing is, I didn't think they'd have their horns so soon. Bernice, I had to, that's all. There'd only been a couple of cats and a — well, sure they chased me, but I — well, Momma, Bernice, what did you want me to do? Just what did you want me to do? You're always so dramatic — why do I shout? I shout because I can't get you to listen to me any other way. You remember what Dr. Schechtman said — what? No, I told you, I just forgot to call. No, that is the reason, that's the real and only reason. Well, whose fault is that? What? Oh, Bernice. Jesus Christ, Bernice. All right, *how* is it Dad's fault?"

She didn't want the coffee, or any breakfast, but she sat at the table in his bathrobe and drank milk greedily. It was the first time he had ever seen her drink milk. Her face was sandy-pale, and her eyes were red. Talking to her mother left her looking as though she had actually gone ten rounds with the woman. Farrell asked, "How long has it been happening?"

"Nine years," Lila said. "Since I hit puberty. First day, cramps; the second day, this. My introduction to womanhood." She snickered and spilled her milk. "I want some more," she said. "Got to get rid of that taste."

"Who knows about it?" he asked. "Pat and Janet?" They were the two girls she had been rooming with.

"God, no. I'd never tell them. I've never told a girl. Bernice knows, of course, and Dr. Schechtman — he's my head doctor. And you now. That's all." Farrell waited. She was a bad liar, and only did it to heighten the effect of the truth. "Well, there was Mickey," she said. "The guy I told you about the first night, you remember? It doesn't matter. He's an acidhead in Vancouver, of all places. He'll never tell anybody."

He thought: I wonder if any girl has ever talked about me in that sort of voice. I doubt it, offhand. Lila said, "It wasn't too hard to keep it a secret. I missed a lot of things. Like I never could go to the riding camp, and I still want to. And the senior play, when I was in high school. They picked me to play the girl in *Liliom*, but then they changed the evening, and I had to say I was sick. And the winter's bad, because the sun sets so early. But actually, it's been a lot less trouble than my goddamn allergies." She made a laugh, but Farrell did not respond.

"Dr. Schechtman says it's a sex thing," she offered. "He says it'll take years and years to cure it. Bernice thinks I should go to someone else, but I don't want to be one of those women who runs around changing shrinks like hair colors. Pat went through five of them in a month one time. Joe, I wish you'd say something. Or just go away."

"Is it only dogs?" he asked. Lila's face did not change, but her chair rattled, and the milk went over again. Farrell said, "Answer me. Do you only kill dogs, and cats, and zoo animals?"

The tears began to come, heavy and slow, bright as knives in the morning sunlight. She could not look at him; and when she tried to speak she could only make creaking, cartilaginous sounds in her throat. "*You* don't know," she whispered at last. "You don't have any idea what it's like."

"That's true," he answered. He was always very fair about that particular point.

He took her hand, and then she really began to cry. Her sobs were horrible to hear, much more frightening to Farrell than any wolf noises. When he held her, she rolled in his arms like a stranded ship with the waves slamming into her. I always get the criers, he thought sadly. My girls always cry, sooner or later. But never for me.

"Don't leave me!" she wept. "I don't know why I came to live with you — I knew it wouldn't work — but don't leave me! There's just Bernice and Dr. Schechtman, and it's so lonely. I want somebody else, I get so lonely. Don't leave me, Joe. I love you, Joe. I love you."

She was patting his face as though she were blind. Farrell stroked her hair and kneaded the back of her neck, wishing that her mother would call again. He felt skilled and weary, and without desire. I'm doing it again, he thought. "I love you," Lila said. And he answered her, thinking, I'm doing it again. That's the great advantage of making the same mistake a lot of times. You come to know it, and you can study it and get inside it, really make it yours. It's the same good old mistake, except this time the girl's hang-up is different. But it's the same thing. I'm doing it again.

The building superintendent was thirty or fifty: dark, thin, quick, and shivering. A Lithuanian or a Latvian, he spoke very little English. He smelled of black friction tape and stale water, and he was strong in the twisting way that a small, lean animal is strong. His eyes were almost purple, and they bulged a little, straining out — the terrible eyes of a herald angel stricken dumb. He roamed the basement all day, banging on pipes and taking the elevator apart.

The superintendent met Lila only a few hours after Farrell did; on that first night, when she came home with him. At the sight of her the little man jumped back, dropping the two-legged chair he was carrying. He promptly fell over it, and did not try to get up, but cowered there, clucking and gulping, trying to cross himself and make the sign of the horns at the same time. Farrell started to help him, but he screamed. They could hardly hear the sound.

It would have been merely funny and embarrassing, except for the fact that Lila was equally frightened of the superintendent, from that moment. She would not go down to the basement for any reason, nor would she enter or leave the house until she was satisfied that he was nowhere near. Farrell had thought then that she took the superintendent for a lunatic.

"I don't know how he knows," he said to Ben. "I guess if you believe in werewolves and vampires, you probably recognize them right away. I don't believe in them at all, and I live with one."

He lived with Lila all through the autumn and the winter. They went out together and came home, and her cooking improved slightly, and she gave up the guitar and got a kitten named Theodora. Sometimes she wept, but not often. She turned out not to be a real crier.

She told Dr. Schechtman about Farrell, and he said that it would probably be a very beneficial relationship for her. It wasn't, but it wasn't a particularly bad one either. Their lovemaking was usually good, though it bothered Farrell to suspect that it was the sense and smell of the Other that excited him. For the rest, they came near being friends. Farrell had known that he did not love Lila before he found out that she was a werewolf, and this made him feel a great deal easier about being bored with her.

"It'll break up by itself in the spring," he said, "like ice."

Ben asked, "What if it doesn't?" They were having lunch in the Automat again. "What'll you do if it just goes on?"

"It's not that easy." Farrell looked away from his friend and began to explore the mysterious, swampy innards of his beef pie. He said, "The trouble is that I know her. That was the real mistake. You shouldn't get to know people if you know you're not going to stay with them, one way or another. It's all right if you come and go in ignorance, but you shouldn't know them."

A week or so before the full moon, she would start to become nervous and strident, and this would continue until the day preceding her transformation. On that day, she was invariably loving, in the tender, desperate manner of someone who is going away; but the next day would see her silent, speaking only when she had to. She always had a cold on the last day, and looked grey and patchy and sick, but she usually went to work anyway.

Farrell was sure, though she never talked about it, that the change into wolf shape was actually peaceful for her, though the returning hurt. Just before moonrise she would take off her clothes and take the pins out of her hair, and stand waiting. Farrell never managed not to close his eyes when she dropped heavily down on all fours; but there was a moment before that when her face would grow a look that he never saw at any other time, except when they were making love. Each time he saw it, it struck him as a look of wondrous joy at not being Lila anymore.

"See, I know her," he tried to explain to Ben. "She only likes to go to color movies, because wolves can't see color. She can't stand the Modern Jazz Quartet, but that's all she plays the first couple of days afterward. Stupid things like that. Never gets high at parties, because she's afraid she'll start talking. It's hard to walk away, that's all. Taking what I know with me."

Ben asked, "Is she still scared of the super?"

"Oh, God," Farrell said. "She got his dog last time. It was a Dalmatian — good-looking animal. She didn't know it was his. He doesn't hide when he sees her now, he just gives her a look like a stake through the heart. That man is a really classy hater, a natural. I'm scared of him myself." He stood up and began to pull on his overcoat. "I wish he'd get turned on to her mother. Get some practical use out of him. Did I tell you she wants me to call her Bernice?"

Ben said, "Farrell, if I were you, I'd leave the country. I would."

They went out into the February drizzle that sniffled back and forth between snow and rain. Farrell did not speak until they reached the corner where he turned towards the bookstore. Then he said very softly, "Damn, you have to be so careful. Who wants to know what people turn into?"

May came, and a night when Lila once again stood naked at the window, waiting for the moon. Farrell fussed with dishes and garbage bags and fed the cat. These moments were always awkward. He had just asked her, "You want to save what's left of the rice?" when the telephone rang.

It was Lila's mother. She called two and three times a week now. "This is Bernice. How's my Irisher this evening?"

"I'm fine, Bernice," Farrell said. Lila suddenly threw back her head and drew a heavy, whining breath. The cat hissed silently and ran into the bathroom.

"I called to inveigle you two uptown this Friday," Mrs. Braun said. "A couple of old friends are coming over, and I know if I don't get some young people in we'll just sit around and talk about what went wrong with the Progressive Party. The Old Left. So if you could sort of sweet-talk our girl into spending an evening in Squaresville —"

"I'll have to check with Lila." She's *doing* it, he thought, that terrible woman. Every time I talk to her, I sound married. I see what she's doing, but she goes right ahead anyway. He said, "I'll talk to her in the morning." Lila struggled in the moonlight, between dancing and drowning. "Oh," Mrs. Braun said. "Yes, of course. Have her call me back." She sighed. "It's such a comfort to me to know you're there. Ask her if I should fix a fondue?"

Lila made a handsome wolf: tall and broad-chested for a female, moving as easily as water sliding over stone. Her coat was dark brown, showing red in the proper light, and there were white places on her breast. She had pale green eyes, the color of the sky when a hurricane is coming. Usually she was gone as soon as the changing was over, for she never cared for him to see her in her wolf form. But tonight she came slowly towards him, walking in a strange way, with her hindquarters almost dragging. She was making a high, soft sound, and her eyes were not focusing on him.

"What is it?" he asked foolishly. The wolf whined and skulked under the table, rubbing against his leg. Then she lay on her belly and rolled and as she did so the sound grew in her throat until it became an odd, sad, thin cry; not a hunting howl, but a shiver of longing turned into breath. "Jesus, don't do that!" Farrell gasped. But she sat up and howled again, and a dog answered her from somewhere near the river. She wagged her tail and whimpered.

Farrell said, "The super'll be up here in two minutes flat. What's the matter with you?" He heard footsteps and low frightened voices in the apartment above them. Another dog howled, this one nearby, and the wolf wriggled a little way towards the window on her haunches, like a baby, scooting. She looked at him over her shoulder, shuddering violently. On an impulse, he picked up the phone and called her mother.

Watching the wolf as she rocked and slithered and moaned, he described her actions to Mrs. Braun. "I've never seen her like this," he said. "I don't know what's the matter with her."

"Oh, my God," Mrs. Braun whispered. She told him.

When he was silent, she began to speak very rapidly. "It hasn't happened for such a long time. Schechtman gives her pills, but she must have run out and forgotten — she's always been like that, since she was little. All the thermos bottles she used to leave on the school bus, and every week her piano music — "

"I wish you'd told me before," he said. He was edging very cautiously towards the open window. The pupils of the wolf's eyes were pulsing with her quick breaths.

"It isn't a thing you tell people!" Lila's mother wailed in his ear. "How do you think it was for me when she brought her first little boyfriend — " Farrell dropped the phone and sprang for the window. He had the inside track, and he might have made it, but she turned her head and snarled so wildly that he fell back. When he reached the window, she was already two fire-escape landings below, and there was eager yelping waiting for her in the street.

Dangling and turning just above the floor, Mrs. Braun heard Farrell's distant yell, followed immediately by a heavy thumping on the door. A strange, tattered voice was shouting unintelligibly beyond the knocking. Footsteps crashed by the receiver and the door opened.

"My dog, my dog!" the strange voice mourned. "My dog, my dog, my dog!"

"I'm sorry about your dog," Farrell said. "Look, please go away. I've got work to do."

"I got work," the voice said. "I know my work." It climbed and spilled into another language, out of which English words jutted like broken bones. "Where is she? Where is she? She kill my dog."

"She's not here." Farrell's own voice changed on the last word. It seemed a long time before he said, "You'd better put that away."

Mrs. Braun heard the howl as clearly as though the wolf were running beneath her own window: lonely and insatiable, with a kind of gasping laughter in it. The other voice began to scream. Mrs. Braun caught the phrase *silver bullet* several times. The door slammed; then opened and slammed again.

Farrell was the only man of his own acquaintance who was able to play back his dreams while he was having them: to stop them in mid-flight, no matter how fearful they might be — or how lovely — and run them over and over studying them in his sleep, until the most terrifying reel became at once utterly harmless and unbearably familiar. This night that he spent running after Lila was like that.

He would find them congregated under the marquee of an apartment house, or romping around the moonscape of a construction site: ten or fifteen males of all races, creeds, colors, and previous conditions of servitude; whining and yapping, pissing against tires, inhaling indiscriminately each other and the lean, grinning bitch they surrounded. She frightened them, for she growled more wickedly than coyness demanded, and where she snapped, even in play, bone showed.

Still they tumbled on her and over her, biting her neck and ears in their turn; and she snarled but she did not run away.

Never, at least, until Farrell came charging upon them, shrieking like any cuckold, kicking at the snuffling lovers. Then she would turn and race off into the spring dark, with her thin, dreamy howl floating behind her like the train of a smoky gown. The dogs followed, and so did Farrell, calling and cursing. They always lost him quickly, that jubilant marriage procession, leaving him stumbling down rusty iron ladders into places where he fell over garbage cans. Yet he would come upon them as inevitably in time, loping along Broadway or trotting across Columbus Avenue towards the Park; he would hear them in the tennis courts near the river, breaking down the nets over Lila and her moment's Ares. There were dozens of them now, coming from all directions. They stank of their joy, and he threw stones at them and shouted, and they ran.

And the wolf ran at their head, on sidewalks and on wet grass; her tail waving contentedly, but her eyes still hungry, and her howl growing ever more warning than wistful. Farrell knew that she must have blood before sunrise, and that it was both useless and dangerous to follow her. But the night wound and unwound itself, and he knew the same things over and over, and ran down the same streets, and saw the same couples walk wide of him, thinking he was drunk.

Mrs. Braun kept leaping out of a taxi that pulled up next to him; usually at corners where the dogs had just piled by, knocking over the crates stacked in market doorways and spilling the newspapers at the subway kiosks. Standing in broccoli, in black taffeta, with a front like a ferry-boat — yet as lean in the hips as her wolf-daughter — with her plum-colored hair all loose, one arm lifted, and her orange mouth pursed in a bellow, she was no longer Bernice but a wronged fertility goddess getting set to blast the harvest. "We've got to split up!" she would roar at Farrell, and each time it sounded like a sound idea. Yet he looked for her whenever he lost Lila's trail, because she never did.

The superintendent kept turning up too, darting after Farrell out of alleys or cellar entrances, or popping from the freight elevators that load through the sidewalk. Farrell would hear his numberless passkeys clicking on the flat piece of wood tucked into his belt.

"You see her? You see her, the wolf, kill my dog?" Under the fat, ugly moon, the Army .45 glittered and trembled like his own mad eyes.

"Mark with a cross." He would pat the barrel of his gun and shake it under Farrell's nose like a maraca. "Mark with a cross, bless by a priest. Three silver bullets. She kill my dog."

Lila's voice would come sailing to them then, from up in Harlem or away near Lincoln Center, and the little man would whirl and dash down into the earth, disappearing into the crack between two slabs of sidewalk. Farrell understood quite clearly that the superintendent was hunting Lila underground, using the keys that only superintendents have to take elevators down to the black sub-sub-basements, far below the bicycle rooms and the wet, shaking laundry rooms, and below the furnace rooms, below the passages walled with electricity meters and roofed with burly steam pipes; down to the realms where the great dim water mains roll like whales, and the gas lines hump and preen, down where the roots of the apartment houses fade together, and so along under the city, scrabbling through secret ways with silver bullets, and his keys rapping against the piece of wood. He never saw Lila, but he was never very far behind her.

Cutting across parking lots, pole-vaulting between locked bumpers, edging and dancing his way through fluorescent gaggles of haughty children; leaping uptown like a salmon against the current of the theatre crowds; walking quickly past the random killing faces that floated down the night tide like unexploded mines, and especially avoiding the crazy faces that wanted to tell him what it was like to be crazy — so Farrell pursued Lila Braun, of Tremont Avenue and CCNY, in the city all night long. Nobody offered to help him, or tried to head off the dangerous-looking bitch bounding along with the delirious gaggle of admirers streaming after her; but then, the dogs had to fight through the same clenched legs and vengeful bodies that Farrell did. The crowds slowed Lila down, but he felt relieved whenever she turned towards the emptier streets. *She must have blood soon, somewhere.*

Farrell's dreams eventually lost their clear edge after he played them back a certain number of times, and so it was with the night. The full moon skidded down the sky, thinning like a tatter of butter in a skillet, and remembered scenes began to fold sloppily into each other. The sound of Lila and the dogs grew fainter whichever way he followed. Mrs. Braun blinked on and off at longer intervals; and in dark doorways and under subway gratings, the superintendent burned like a corposant, making the barrel of his pistol run rainbow. At last he lost Lila for good, and with that it seemed that he woke.

It was still night, but not dark, and he was walking slowly home on

Riverside Drive through a cool, grainy fog. The moon had set, but the river was strangely bright: glittering grey as far up as the Bridge, where headlights left shiny, wet paths like snails. There was no one else on the street. "Dumb broad," he said aloud. "The hell with it. She wants to mess around, let her mess around." He wondered whether werewolves could have cubs, and what sort of cubs they might be. Lila must have turned on the dogs by now, for the blood. Poor dogs, he thought. They were all so dirty and innocent and happy with her.

"A moral lesson for all of us," he announced sententiously. "Don't fool with strange, eager ladies, they'll kill you." He was a little hysterical. Then, two blocks ahead of him, he saw the gaunt shape in the grey light of the river; alone now, and hurrying. Farrell did not call to her, but as soon as he began to run, the wolf wheeled and faced him. Even at that distance, her eyes were stained and streaked and wild. She showed all the teeth on one side of her mouth, and she growled like fire.

Farrell trotted steadily towards her, crying, "Go home, go home! Lila, you dummy, get on home, it's morning!" She growled terribly, but when Farrell was less than a block away she turned again and dashed across the street, heading for West End Avenue. Farrell said, "Good girl, that's it," and limped after her.

In the hours before sunrise on West End Avenue, many people came out to walk their dogs. Farrell had done it often enough with poor Grunewald to know many of the dawn walkers by sight, and some to talk to. A fair number of them were whores and homosexuals, both of whom always seem to have dogs in New York. Quietly, almost always alone, they drifted up and down the Nineties, piloted by their small, fussy beasts, but moving in a kind of fugitive truce with the city and the night that was ending. Farrell sometimes fancied that they were all asleep, and that this hour was the only true rest they ever got.

He recognized Robie by his two dogs, Scone and Crumpet. Robie lived in the apartment directly below Farrell's, usually unhappily. The dogs were horrifying little homebrews of Chihuahua and Yorkshire terrier, but Robie loved them.

Crumpet, the male, saw Lila first. He gave a delighted yap of welcome and proposition (according to Robie, Scone bored him, and he liked big girls anyway) and sprang to meet her, yanking his leash through Robie's slack hand. The wolf was almost upon him before he realized his fatal misunderstanding and scuttled desperately in retreat, meowing with utter terror.

Robie wailed, and Farrell ran as fast as he could, but Lila knocked Crumpet off his feet and slashed his throat while he was still in the air. Then she crouched on the body, nuzzling it in a dreadful way.

Robie actually came within a step of leaping upon Lila and trying to drag her away from his dead dog. Instead, he turned on Farrell as he came panting up, and began hitting him with a good deal of strength and accuracy. "Damn you, damn you!" he sobbed. Little Scone ran away around the corner, screaming like a mandrake.

Farrell put up his arms and went with the punches, all the while yelling at Lila until his voice ripped. But the blood frenzy had her, and Farrell never imagined what she must be like at those times. Somehow she had spared the dogs who had loved her all night, but she was nothing but thirst now. She pushed and kneaded Crumpet's body as though she were nursing.

All along the avenue, the morning dogs were barking like trumpets. Farrell ducked away from Robie's soft fists and saw them coming; tripping over their trailing leashes, running too fast for their stubby legs. They were small, spoiled beasts, most of them, overweight and shortwinded, and many were not young. Their owners cried unmanly pet names after them, but they waddled gallantly towards their deaths, barking promises far bigger than themselves, and none of them looked back.

She looked up with her muzzle red to the eyes. The dogs did falter then, for they knew murder when they smelled if, and even their silly, nearsighted eyes understood vaguely what creature faced them. But they knew the smell of love too, and they were all gentlemen.

She killed the first two to reach her — a spitz and a cocker spaniel — with two snaps of her jaws. But before she could settle down to her meal, three Pekes were scrambling up to her, though they would have had to stand on each other's shoulders. Lila whirled without a sound, and they fell away, rolling and yelling but unhurt. As soon as she turned, the Pekes were at her again, joined now by a couple of valiant poodles. Lila got one of the poodles when she turned again. Robie had stopped beating on Farrell, and was leaning against a traffic light, being sick. But other people were running up now: a middle-aged black man, crying; a plump youth in a plastic car coat and bedroom slippers, who kept whimpering, "Oh God, she's eating them, look at her, she's really eating them!"; two lean, ageless girls in slacks, both with foamy beige hair. They all called wildly to their unheeding dogs, and they all grabbed at

Farrell and shouted in his face. Cars began to stop.

The sky was thin and cool, rising pale gold, but Lila paid no attention to it. She was ramping under the swarm of little dogs; rearing and spinning in circles, snarling blood. The dogs were terrified and bewildered, but they never swerved from their labor. The smell of love told them that they were welcome, however ungraciously she seemed to receive them. Lila shook herself, and a pair of squealing dachshunds, hobbled in a double harness, tumbled across the sidewalk to end at Farrell's feet. They scrambled up and immediately towed themselves back into the maelstrom. Lila bit one of them almost in half, but the other dachshund went on trying to climb her hindquarters, dragging his ripped comrade with him. Farrell began to laugh.

The black man said, "You think it's funny?" and hit him. Farrell sat down, still laughing. The man stood over him, embarrassed, offering Farrell his handkerchief. "I'm sorry, I shouldn't have done that," he said. "But your dog killed my dog."

"She isn't my dog," Farrell said. He moved to let a man pass between them, and then saw that it was the superintendent, holding his pistol with both hands. Nobody noticed him until he fired; but Farrell pushed one of the foamy-haired girls, and she stumbled against the superintendent as the gun went off. The silver bullet broke a window in a parked car.

The superintendent fired again while the echoes of the first shot were still clapping back and forth between the houses. A Pomeranian screamed that time, and a woman cried out, "Oh my God, he shot Borgy!" But the crowd was crumbling away, breaking into its individual components like pills on television. The watching cars had sped off at the sight of the gun, and the faces that had been peering down from windows disappeared. Except for Farrell, the few people who remained were scattered halfway down the block. The sky was brightening swiftly now.

"For God's sake, don't let him!" the same woman called from the shelter of a doorway. But two men made shushing gestures at her, saying, "It's all right, he knows how to use that thing. Go ahead, buddy."

The shots had at last frightened the little dogs away from Lila. She crouched among the twitching splotches of fur, with her muzzle wrinkled back and her eyes more black than green. Farrell saw a plaid rag that had been a dog jacket protruding from under her body. The superintendent stooped and squinted over the gun barrel, aiming with grotesque care, while the men cried to him to shoot. He was too far from the werewolf for her to reach him before he fired the last silver bullet, though he would surely die before she died. His lips were moving as he took aim.

Two long steps would have brought Farrell up behind the superintendent. Later he told himself that he had been afraid of the pistol, because that was easier than remembering how he had felt when he looked at Lila. Her tongue never stopped lapping around her dark jaws; and even as she set herself to spring, she lifted a bloody paw to her mouth. Farrell thought of her padding in the bedroom, breathing on his face. The superintendent grunted and Farrell closed his eyes. Yet even then he expected to find himself doing something.

Then he heard Mrs. Braun's unmistakable voice. *"Don't you dare!"* She was standing between Lila and the superintendent: one shoe gone, and the heel off the other one; her knit dress torn at the shoulder, and her face tired and smudgy. But she pointed a finger at the startled superintendent, and he stepped quickly back, as though she had a pistol, too.

"Lady, that's a wolf," he protested nervously. "Lady, you please get, get out of the way. That's a wolf, I go shoot her now."

"I want to see your license for that gun." Mrs. Braun held out her hand. The superintendent blinked at her, muttering in despair. She said, "Do you know that you can be sent to prison for twenty years for carrying a concealed weapon in this state? Do you know what the fine is for having a gun without a license? The fine is Five. Thousand. Dollars." The men down the street were shouting at her, but she swung around to face the creature snarling among the little dead dogs.

"Come on, Lila," she said. "Come on home with Bernice. I'll make tea and we'll talk. It's been a long time since we've really talked, you know? We used to have nice long talks when you were little, but we don't anymore." The wolf had stopped growling, but she was crouching even lower, and her ears were still flat against her head. Mrs. Braun said, "Come on, baby. Listen, I know what — you'll call in sick at the office and stay for a few days. You'll get a good rest, and maybe we'll even look around a little for a new doctor, what do you say? Schechtman hasn't done a thing for you, I never liked him. Come on home, honey. Momma's here, Bernice knows." She took a step towards the silent wolf, holding out her hand.

The superintendent gave a desperate, wordless cry and pumped forward, clumsily shoving Mrs. Braun to one side. He leveled the pistol point-blank, wailing, "My dog, my dog!" Lila was in the air when the gun went off, and her shadow sprang after her, for the sun had risen. She crumpled down across a couple of dead Pekes. Their blood dabbled her breasts and her pale throat.

Mrs. Braun screamed like a lunch whistle. She knocked the superintendent into the street and sprawled over Lila, hiding her completely from Farrell's sight. "Lila, Lila," she keened to her daughter, "poor baby, you never had a chance. He killed you because you were different, the way they kill everything different." Farrell approached her and stooped down, but she pushed him against a wall without looking up. "Lila, Lila, poor baby, poor darling, maybe it's better, maybe you're happy now. You never had a chance, poor Lila."

The dog owners were edging slowly back and the surviving dogs were running to them. The superintendent squatted on the curb with his head in his arms. A wary, muffled voice said, "For God's sake, Bernice, would you get up off me? You don't have to stop yelling, just get off."

When she stood up, the cars began to stop in the street again. It made it very difficult for the police to get through. Nobody pressed charges, because there was no one to lodge them against. The killer dog — or wolf, as some insisted — was gone; and if she had an owner, he could not be found. As for the people who had actually seen the wolf turn into a young girl when the sunlight touched her; most of them managed not to have seen it, though they never really forgot. There were a few who knew quite well what they had seen, and never forgot it either, but they never said anything. They did, however, chip in to pay the superintendent's fine for possessing an unlicensed handgun. Farrell gave what he could.

Lila vanished out of Farrell's life before sunset. She did not go uptown with her mother, but packed her things and went to stay with friends in the Village. Later he heard that she was living on Christopher Street; and later still, that she had moved to Berkeley and gone back to school. He never saw her again.

"It had to be like that," he told Ben once. "We got to know too much about each other. See, there's another side to knowing. She couldn't look at me."

"You mean because you saw her with all those dogs? Or because she knew you'd have let that little nut shoot her?" Farrell shook his head.

"It was that, I guess, but it was more something else, something I know. When she sprang, just as he shot at her that last time, she wasn't leaping at him. She was going straight for her mother. She'd have got her too, if it hadn't been sunrise."

Ben whistled softly. "I wonder if her old lady knows."

"Bernice knows everything about Lila," Farrell said.

Mrs. Braun called him nearly two years later to tell him that Lila was getting married. It must have cost her a good deal of money and ingenuity to find him (where Farrell was living then, the telephone line was open for four hours a day), but he knew by the spitefulness in the static that she considered it money well spent.

"He's at Stanford," she crackled. "A research psychologist. They're going to Japan for their honeymoon."

"That's fine," Farrell said. "I'm really happy for her, Bernice." He hesitated before he asked, "Does he know about Lila? I mean, about what happens — ?"

"Does he know?" she cried. "He's proud of it — he thinks it's wonderful! It's his field!"

"That's great. That's fine. Goodbye, Bernice. I really am glad."

And he was glad, and a little wistful, thinking about it. The girl he was living with here had a really strange hangup.

Julie's Unicorn

The note came with the entree, tucked neatly under the zucchini slices but carefully out of range of the seafood crepes. It said, in the unmistakable handwriting that any graphologist would have ascribed to a serial killer, "Tanikawa, ditch the dork and get in here." Julie took her time over the crepes and the spinach salad, finished her wine, sampled a second glass, and then excused herself to her dinner partner, who smiled and propped his chin on his fingertips, prepared to wait graciously, as assistant professors know how to do. She turned right at the telephones, instead of left, looked back once, and walked through a pair of swinging half-doors into the restaurant kitchen.

The heat thumped like a fist between her shoulder blades, and her glasses fogged up immediately. She took them off, put them in her purse and focused on a slender, graying man standing with his back to her as he instructed an earnest young woman about shiitake mushroom stew. Julie said loudly, "Make it quick, Farrell. The dork thinks I'm in the can."

The slender man said to the young woman, "Gracie, tell Luis the basil's losing its marbles, he can put in more oregano if he wants. Tell him to use his own judgment about the lemongrass — I like it myself." Then he turned, held out his arms and said, "Jewel. Think you strung it out long enough?"

"My dessert's melting," Julie said into his apron. The arms around her felt as comfortably usual as an old sofa, and she lifted her head quickly to demand, "God damn it, where have you been? I have had very strange phone conversations with some very strange people in the last five years, trying to track you down. What the hell happened to you, Farrell?"

"What happened to me? Two addresses and a fax number I gave you, and nothing. Not a letter, not so much as a postcard from East Tarpit-on-the-Orinoco, hi, marrying tribal chieftain tomorrow, wish you were here. But just as glad you're not. The story of this relationship."

Julie stepped back, her round, long-eyed face gone as pale as it ever got. Almost in a whisper, she asked, "How did you know? Farrell, how did you know?" The young cook was staring at them both in fascination bordering on religious rapture.

"What?" Farrell said, and now he was gaping like the cook, his own voice snagging in his throat. "You did? You got married?"

"It didn't last. Eight months. He's in Boston."

"That explains it." Farrell's sudden bark of laughter made Gracie the cook jump slightly. "By God, that explains it."

"Boston? Boston explains what?"

"You didn't want me to know," Farrell said. "You really didn't want me to know. Tanikawa, I'm ashamed of you. I am."

Julie started to answer him, then nodded toward the entranced young cook. Farrell said, "Gracie, about the curried peas. Tell Suzanne absolutely not to add the mango pickle until just before the peas are done, she always puts it in too early. If she's busy, you do it — go, go." Gracie, enchanted even more by the notion of getting her hands into actual food, fled, and Farrell turned back to face Julie. "Eight months. I've known you to take longer over a lithograph."

"He's a very nice man," she answered him. "No, damn it, that sounds terrible, insulting. But he is."

Farrell nodded. "I believe it. You always did have this deadly weakness for nice men. I was an aberration."

"No, you're my friend," Julie said. "You're my friend, and I'm sorry, I should have told you I was getting married." A waiter's loaded tray caught her between the shoulderblades just as a busboy stepped on her foot, and she was properly furious this time. "I didn't tell you because I knew you'd do exactly what you're doing now, which is look at me like that and imply that you know me better than anyone else ever possibly could, which is not true, Farrell. There are all kinds of people you don't even know who know things about me you'll never know, so just knock it off." She ran out of breath and anger more or less simultaneously. She said, "But somehow you've gotten to be my oldest friend, just by goddamn attrition. I missed you, Joe."

Farrell put his arms around her again. "I missed you. I worried about you. A whole lot. The rest can wait." There came a crash and a mad bellow from the steamy depths of the kitchen, and Farrell said, "Your dork's probably missing you too. That was the Table Fourteen dessert, sure as hell. Where can I call you? Are you actually back in Avicenna?"

"For now. It's always for now in this town." She wrote the address and telephone number on the back of the Tonight's Specials menu, kissed him hurriedly and left the kitchen. Behind her she heard another bellow, and then Farrell's grimly placid voice saying, "Stay cool, stay cool, big Luis, it's not the end of the world. Change your apron, we'll just add some more brandy. All is well."

It took more time than they were used to, even after more than twenty years of picking up, letting go and picking up again. The period of edginess and uncertainty about what questions to ask, what to leave alone, what might or might not be safe to assume, lasted until the autumn afternoon they went to the museum. It was Farrell's day off, and he drove Madame Schumann-Heink, his prehistoric Volkswagen van, over the hill from the bald suburb where he was condo-sitting for a friend and parked under a sycamore across from Julie's studio apartment. The building was a converted Victorian, miraculously spared from becoming a nest of suites for accountants and attorneys and allowed to decay in a decently tropical fashion, held together by jasmine and wisteria. He said to Julie, "You find trees, every time, shady places with big old trees. I've never figured how you manage it."

"Old houses," she said. "I always need work space and a lot of light, and only the old houses have it. It's a trade-off — plumbing for elbow room. Wait till I feed NMC." NMC was an undistinguished black and white cat who slept with six new kittens in a box underneath the tiny sink set into a curtained alcove. ("She likes to keep an eye on the refrigerator," Julie explained. "Just in case it tries to make a break for freedom.") She had shown up pregnant, climbing the stairs to scratch only at Julie's door, and sauntering in with an air of being specifically expected. The initials of her name stood for Not My Cat. Julie opened a can, set it down beside the box, checked to make sure that each kitten was securely attached to a nipple, briefly fondled a softly thrumming throat and told her, "The litter tray is two feet to your left. As if you care."

At the curb, gazing for a long time at Madame Schumann-Heink, she said, "This thing has become absolutely transparent, Joe, you know that. I can see the Bay right through it."

"Wait till you see her by moonlight," Farrell said. "Gossamer and cobwebs. The Taj Mahal of rust. Tell me again where the Bigby Museum is."

"North. East. In the hills. It's hard to explain. Take the freeway, I'll tell you where to turn off."

The Bigby City Museum had been, until fairly recently, Avicenna's nearest approach to a Roman villa. Together with its long, narrow reflecting pool and its ornamental gardens, it occupied an entire truncated hilltop from which, morning and evening, its masters — copper-mining kinglets — had seen the Golden Gate Bridge rising through the Bay mist like a Chinese dragon's writhing back. With the death of the last primordial Bigby, the lone heir had quietly sold the mansion to the city, set up its contents (primarily lesser works of the lesser Impressionists, a scattering of the Spanish masters, and the entire oeuvre of a Bigby who painted train stations) as a joint trust, and sailed away to a tax haven in the Lesser Antilles. Julie said there were a few early Brueghel oils and drawings worth the visit. "He was doing Bosch then — maybe forgeries, maybe not — and mostly you can't tell them apart. But with these you start seeing the real Brueghel, sort of in spite of himself. There's a good little Raphael too, but you'll hate it. An Annunciation, with *putti*."

"I'll hate it," Farrell said. He eased Madame Schumann-Heink over into the right-hand lane, greatly irritating a BMW, who honked at him all the way to the freeway. "Practically as much as I hate old whoever, the guy you married."

"Brian." Julie punched his shoulder hard. "His name is Brian, and he's a lovely, wonderful man, and I really do love him. We just shouldn't have gotten married. We both agreed on that."

"A damn Brian," Farrell said. He put his head out of the window and yelled back at the BMW, "She went and married a Brian, I ask you!" The BMW driver gave him the finger. Farrell said, "The worst thing is, I'd probably like him, I've got a bad feeling about that. Let's talk about something else. Why'd you marry him?"

Julie sighed. "Maybe because he was as far away from you as I could get. He's sane, he's stable, he's — okay, he's ambitious, nothing wrong with that —"

Farrell's immediate indignation surprised him as much as it did Julie. "Hey, I'm sane. All things considered. Weird is not wacko, there's a fine but definite line. And I'm stable as a damn lighthouse, or we'd never have stayed friends this long. Ambitious — okay, no, never, not really. Still cooking here and there, still playing a bit of obsolete music on obsolete instruments after hours. Same way you're still drawing cross sections of lungs and livers for medical students. What does old ambitious Brian do?"

"He's a lawyer." Julie heard herself mumbling, saw the corner of Farrell's mouth twitch, and promptly flared up again. "And I don't want to hear one bloody word out of you, Farrell! He's not a hired gun for corporations, he doesn't defend celebrity gangsters. He works for non-profits, environmental groups, refugees, gay rights — he takes on so many pro bono cases, half the time he can't pay his office rent. He's a better person than you'll ever be, Farrell. Or me either. That's the damn, damn trouble." Her eyes were aching heavily, and she looked away from him.

Farrell put his hand gently on the back of her neck. He said, "I'm sorry, Jewel." Neither of them spoke after that until they were grinding slowly up a narrow street lined with old sycamore and walnut trees and high, furry old houses drowsing in the late-summer sun. Julie said, "I do a little word-processing, temp stuff," and then, in the same flat voice, "You never married anybody."

"Too old," Farrell said. "I used to be too young, or somebody was, I remember that. Now it's plain too late — I'm me, finally, all the way down, and easy enough with it, but I damn sure wouldn't marry me." He braked to keep from running over two cackling adolescents on skateboards, then resumed the lumbering climb, dropping Madame Schumann-Heink into second gear, which was one of her good ones. Looking sideways, he said, "One thing anyway, you're still the prettiest Eskimo anybody ever saw."

"Get out of here," she answered him scornfully. "You never saw an Eskimo that wasn't in some National Geographic special." Now she looked back at him, fighting a smile, and he touched her neck again, very lightly. "Well, I'm getting like that myself," she said. "Too old and too cranky to suit anybody but me. Turn right at the light, Joe."

The Bigby City Museum came upon them suddenly, filling the windshield just after the last sharp curve, as they rolled slightly downward into a graveled parking lot which had once been an herb garden. Farrell parked facing the Bay, and the two of them got out and stood silently on either side of Madame Schumann-Heink, staring away at the water glittering in the western sun. Then they turned, each with an odd, unspoken near-reluctance, to face the Museum. It would have been a beautiful building, Julie thought, in another town. It was three stories high, cream white, with a flat tile roof the color of red wine. Shadowed on three sides by cypress trees, camellia bushes softening the rectitude of the corners, a dancing-dolphin fountain chuckling in the sunny courtyard, and the white and peach rose gardens sloping away from the reflecting pool, it was a beautiful house, but one that belonged in Santa Barbara, Santa Monica or Malibu, worlds and wars, generations and elections removed from silly, vain, vainly perverse Avicenna. Farrell finally sighed and said, "Power to the people, hey," and Julie said, "*A bas les aristos*," and they went inside. The ticketseller and the guest book were on the first floor, the Brueghels on the second. Julie and Farrell walked up a flowing mahogany stairway hung with watercolors from the Southwestern period of the train-station Bigby. On the landing Farrell looked around judiciously and announced, "Fine command of plastic values, I'll say that," to which Julie responded, "Oh, no question, but those spatio-temporal vortices, I don't know." They laughed together, joined hands and climbed the rest of the way.

There were ten or twelve other people upstairs in the huge main gallery. Most were younger than Farrell and Julie, with the distinct air of art students on assignment, their eyes flicking nervously from the Brueghels to their fellows to see whether anyone else had caught the trick, fathomed the koan, winkled out the grade points that must surely be hiding somewhere within those depictions of demon priests and creatures out of anchorite nightmares. When Julie took a small pad out of her purse, sat down on a couch and began copying certain corners and aspects of the paintings, the students were eddying silently toward her within minutes, just in case she knew. Farrell winked at her and wandered off toward a wall of train stations. Julie never looked up.

More quickly than she expected, he was back, leaning over her shoulder, his low voice in her hair. "Jewel. Something you ought to see. Right around the corner."

The corner was actually a temporary wall, just wide and high enough to hold three tapestries whose placard described them as ". . . mid-fifteenth century, artist unknown, probably from Bruges." The highest tapestry, done in the terrifyingly detailed millefleurs style, showed several women in a rich garden being serenaded by a lute-player, and Julie at first thought that Farrell — a lutanist himself — must have meant her to look at this one. Then she saw the one below.

It was in worse shape than the upper tapestry, badly frayed all around the edges and darkly stained in a kind of rosette close to the center, which showed a knight presenting a unicorn to his simpering lady. The unicorn was small and bluish-white, with the cloven hooves, long neck and slender quarters of a deer. The knight was leading it on a silvery cord, and his squire behind him was prodding the unicorn forward with a short stabbing lance. There was a soapbubble castle in the background, floating up out of a stylized broccoli forest. Julie heard herself say in a child's voice, "I don't like this."

"I've seen better," Farrell agreed. "Wouldn't have picked it as Bruges work myself." The lance was pricking the unicorn hard enough that the flesh dimpled around the point, and the unicorn's one visible eye, purple-black, was rolled back toward the squire in fear or anger. The knight's lady held a wreath of scarlet flowers in her extended right hand. Whether it was meant for the knight or the unicorn Julie could not tell.

"I wish you hadn't shown me this," she said. She turned and returned to the Brueghels, trying to recapture her focus on the sliver of canvas, the precise brushstroke, where the young painter could be seen to step away from his master. But time after time she was drawn back, moving blindly through the growing crowd to stare one more time at the shabby old imagining of beauty and theft before she took up her sketchpad again. At last she gave up any notion of work, and simply stood still before the tapestry, waiting patiently to grow numb to the unicorn's endless woven pain. The lady looked directly out at her, the faded smirk saying clearly, "Five hundred years. Five hundred years, and it is still going on, this very minute, all to the greater glory of God and courtly love."

"That's what you think," Julie said aloud. She lifted her right hand and moved it slowly across the tapestry, barely brushing the protective glass. As she did so, she spoke several words in a language that might have been Japanese, and was not. With the last syllable came a curious muffled jolt, like an underwater explosion, that thudded distantly through her body, making her step back and stagger against Farrell. He gripped her shoulders, saying, "Jewel, what the hell are you up to? What did you just do right then?"

"I don't know what you're talking about," she said, and for that moment it was true. She was oddly dizzy, and she could feel a headache coiling in her temples. "I didn't do anything, what could I do? What do you think I was doing, Joe?"

Farrell turned her to face him, his hands light on her shoulders now, but his dark-blue eyes holding her with an intensity she had rarely seen in all the years they had known each other. He said, "I remember you telling me about your grandmother's Japanese magic. I remember a night really long ago, and a goddess who came when you called her. It all makes me the tiniest bit uneasy."

The strange soft shock did not come again; the art students and the tourists went on drifting as drowsily as aquarium fish among the Brueghels; the figures in the tapestry remained exactly where they had posed for five centuries. Julie said, "I haven't done a damn thing." Farrell's eyes did not leave her face. "Not anything that made any difference, anyway," she said. She turned away and walked quickly across the gallery to examine a very minor Zurbaran too closely.

In time the notepad came back out of her purse, and she again began to copy those scraps and splinters of the Brueghels that held lessons or uses for her. She did not return to the unicorn tapestry. More time passed than she had meant to spend in the museum, and when Farrell appeared beside her she was startled at the stained pallor of the sky outside the high windows. He said, "You better come take a look. That was one hell of a grandmother you had."

She asked no questions when he took hold of her arm and led her — she could feel the effort it cost him not to drag her — back to the wall of tapestries. She stared at the upper one for a long moment before she permitted herself to understand.

The unicorn was gone. The knight and his squire remained in their places, silver cord hauling nothing forward, lance jabbing cruelly into helpless nothing. The lady went on smiling milkily, offering her flowers to nothingness. There was no change in any of their faces, no indication that the absence of the reason for their existence had been noticed at all. Julie stared and stared and said nothing.

"Let you out of my sight for five minutes," Farrell said. He was not looking at her, but scanning the floor in every direction. "All right, main thing's to keep him from getting stepped on. Check the corners — you do that side, I'll do all this side." But he was shaking his head even before he finished. "No, the stairs, you hit the stairs. If he gets down those stairs, that's it, we've lost him. Jewel, go!" He had not raised his voice at all, but the last words cracked like pine sap in fire.

Julie gave one last glance at the tapestry, hoping that the unicorn would prove not to be lost after all, but only somehow absurdly overlooked. But not so much as a dangling thread suggested that there had ever been any other figure in the frame. She said vaguely, "I didn't think it would work, it was just to be doing something," and sprang for the stairway.

By now the art students had been mostly replaced by nuzzling couples and edgy family groups. Some of them grumbled as Julie pushed down past them without a word of apology; a few others turned to gape when she took up a position on the landing, midway between a lost-contact-lens stoop and a catcher's crouch, looking from side to side for some miniature scurry, something like a flittering dust-kitten with a tiny blink at its brow... But will it be flesh, or only dyed yarn? and will it grow to full size, now it's out of the frame? Does it know, does it know it's free, or is it hiding in my shadow, in a thousand times more danger than when there was a rope around its neck and a virgin grinning at it? Grandma, what have we done?

Closing time, nearly, and full dark outside, and still no trace of the unicorn. Julie's heart sank lower with each person who clattered past her down the stairs, and each time the lone guard glanced at her, then at Farrell, and then pointedly wiped his snuffly nose. Farrell commandeered her notepad and prowled the floor, ostentatiously scrutinizing the Brueghels when he felt himself being scrutinized, but studying nothing but dim corners and alcoves the rest of the time. The museum lights were flicking on and off, and the guard had actually begun to say, "Five minutes to closing," when Farrell stopped moving, so suddenly that one foot was actually in the air. Sideways-on to Julie, so that she could not see what he saw, he slowly lowered his foot to the floor; very slowly he turned toward the stair; with the delicacy of a parent maneuvering among Legos, he navigated silently back to her. He was smiling as carefully as though he feared the noise it might make.

"Found it," he muttered. "Way in behind the coat rack, there's a water cooler on an open frame. It's down under there."

"So what are you doing down here?" Julie demanded. Farrell shushed her frantically with his face and hands. He muttered, "It's not going anywhere, it's too scared to move. I need you to distract the guard for a minute. Like in the movies."

"Like in the movies." She sized up the guard: an overage rent-a-cop, soft and bored, interested only in getting them out of the museum, locking up and heading for dinner. "Right. I could start taking my clothes off, there's that. Or I could tell him I've lost my little boy, or maybe ask him what he thinks about fifteenth-century Flemish woodcuts. What are you up to now, Joe?"

"Two minutes," Farrell said. "At the outside. I just don't want the guy to see me grabbing the thing up. Two minutes and gone."

"Hey," Julie said loudly. "Hey, it is not a thing, and you will not grab it." She did lower her voice then, because the guard was glancing at his watch, whistling fretfully. "Joe, I don't know if this has sunk in yet, but a unicorn, a real unicorn, has been trapped in that miserable medieval scene for five centuries, and it is now hiding under a damn water cooler in the Bigby Museum in Avicenna, California. Does that begin to register at all?"

"Trouble," Farrell said. "All that registers is me being in trouble again. Go talk to that man."

Julie settled on asking with breathy shyness about the museum's legendary third floor, always closed off to the public and rumored variously to house the secret Masonic works of Rembrandt, Goya's blasphemous sketches of Black Masses, certain Beardsley illustrations of de Sade, or merely faded pornographic snapshots of assorted Bigby mistresses. The guard's money was on forgeries: counterfeits donated to the city in exchange for handsome tax exemptions. "Town like this, a town full of art experts, specialists — well, you wouldn't want anybody looking at that stuff too close. Stands to reason."

She did not dare look to see what Farrell was doing. The guard was checking his watch again when he appeared beside her, his ancient bomber jacket already on, her coat over his arm. "On our way," he announced cheerfully; and, to the guard, "Sorry for the delay, we're out of here." His free right hand rested, casually but unmoving, on the buttonless flap of his side pocket.

They did not speak on the stairs, nor immediately outside in the autumn twilight. Farrell walked fast, almost pulling her along, until they reached the van. He turned there, his face without expression for a very long moment before he took her hand and brought it to his right coat pocket. Through the cracked leather under her fingers she felt a stillness more vibrant than any struggle could have been: a waiting quiet, making her shiver with a kind of fear and a kind of wonder that she had never known and could not tell apart. She whispered, "Joe, can it — are you sure it can breathe in there?"

"Could it breathe in that damn tapestry?" Farrell's voice was rough and tense, but he touched Julie's hand gently. "It's all right, Jewel. It stood there and looked at me, and sort of watched me picking it up. Let's get on back to your place and figure out what we do now."

Julie sat close to him on the way home, her hand firmly on his coat-pocket flap. She could feel the startlingly intense heat of the unicorn against her palm as completely as though there were nothing between them; she could feel the equally astonishing sharpness of the minute horn, and the steady twitch of the five-century-old heart. As intensely as she could, she sent the thought down her arm and through her fingers: we're going to help you, we're your friends, we know you, don't be afraid. Whenever the van hit a bump or a pothole, she quickly pressed her hand under Farrell's pocket to cushion the legend inside.

Sitting on her bed, their coats still on and kittens meowling under the sink for their absent mother, she said, "All right, we have to think this through. We can't keep it, and we can't just turn it loose in millennial California. What other options do we have?"

"I love it when you talk like a CEO," Farrell said. Julie glared at him. Farrell said, "Well, I'll throw this out to the board meeting. Could you and your grandmother possibly put the poor creature back where you got it? That's what my mother always told me to do."

"Joe, we can't!" she cried out. "We can't put it back into that world, with people capturing it, sticking spears into it for the glory of Christian virginity. I'm not going to do that, I don't care if I have to take care of it for the rest of my life, I'm not going to do that."

"You know you can't take care of it." Farrell took her hands, turned them over, and placed his own hands lightly on them, palm to palm. "As somebody quite properly reminded me a bit back, it's a unicorn."

"Well, we can just set it free." Her throat felt dry, and she realized that her hands were trembling under his. "We'll take it to the wildest national park we can get to — national wilderness, better, no roads, people don't go there — and we'll turn it loose where it belongs. Unicorns live in the wilderness, it would get on fine. It would be happy."

"So would the mountain lions," Farrell said. "And the coyotes and the foxes, and God knows what else. A unicorn the size of a pork chop may be immortal, but that doesn't mean it's indigestible. We do have a problem here, Jewel." They were silent for a long time, looking at each other. Julie said at last, very quietly, "I had to, Joe. I just never thought it would work, but I had to try."

Farrell nodded. Julie was looking, not at him now, but at his coat pocket. She said, "If you put it on the table. Maybe it'll know we don't mean it any harm. Maybe it won't run away."

She leaned forward as Farrell reached slowly into his pocket, unconsciously spreading her arms to left and right, along the table's edge. But the moment Farrell's expression changed she was up and whirling to look in every direction, as she had done on the museum stair. The unicorn was nowhere to be seen. Neither was the cat NMC. The six kittens squirmed and squeaked blindly in their box, trying to suck each other's paws and ears.

Farrell stammered, "I never felt it — I don't know how. . ." and Julie said, "Bathroom, bathroom," and fled there, leaving him forlornly prowling the studio, with its deep, murky fireplace and antique shadows. He was still at it when she returned, empty-handed as he, and her wide eyes fighting wildness.

Very quietly, she said, "I can't find the cat. Joe, I'm scared, I can't find her."

NMC — theatrical as all cats — chose that moment to saunter grandly between them, purring in throaty hiccups, with the unicorn limp between her jaws. Julie's gasp of horror, about to become a scream, was choked off by her realization that the creature was completely unharmed. NMC had it by the back of the neck, exactly as she would have carried one of her kittens, and the purple eyes were open and curiously tranquil. The unicorn's dangling legs — disproportionately long, in the tapestry, for its deerlike body — now seemed to Julie as right as a peach, or the nautilus coil inside each human ear. There was a soft, curling tuft under its chin, less like hair than like feathers, matched by a larger one at the end of its tail. Its hooves and horn had a faint pearl shine, even in the dim light.

Magnificently indifferent to Farrell and Julie's gaping, NMC promenaded to her box, flowed over the side, and sprawled out facing the kittens, releasing her grip on the unicorn's scruff as she did so. It lay passively, legs folded under it, as the squalling mites scrimmaged across their mother's belly. But when Farrell reached cautiously to pick it up, the unicorn's head whipped around faster than any cat ever dreamed of striking, and the horn scored the side of his right hand. Farrell yelped, and Julie said wonderingly, "It wants to be there. It feels comforted with them."

"The sweet thing," Farrell muttered, licking the blood from his hand. The unicorn was shoving its way in among NMC's kittens now: as Julie and Farrell watched, it gently nudged a foster brother over to a nipple next down from the one it had chosen, took the furry tap daintily into its mouth, and let its eyes drift shut. Farrell said it was purring. Julie heard no sound at all from the thin blue-white throat, but she sat by the box long after Farrell had gone home, watching the unicorn's flanks rise and fall in the same rhythm as the kittens' breathing.

Surprisingly, the unicorn appeared perfectly content to remain indefinitely in Julie's studio apartment, living in an increasingly crowded cardboard box among six growing kittens, who chewed on it and slept on it by turns, as they chewed and slept on one another. NMC, for her part, washed it at least twice as much as she bathed any of the others ("To get rid of that nasty old medieval smell," Farrell said), and made a distinct point of sleeping herself with one forepaw plopped heavily across its body. The kittens were not yet capable of climbing out of the box — though they spent most of their waking hours in trying — but NMC plainly sensed that her foster child could come and go as easily as she. Yet, unlike its littermates, the unicorn showed no interest in going anywhere at all.

"Something's wrong," Farrell said after nearly a week. "It's not acting properly — it ought to be wild to get out, wild to be off about its unicorn business. Christ, what if I hurt it when I picked it up in the museum?" His face was suddenly cold and pale. "Jewel, I was so careful, I don't know how I could have hurt it. But I bet that's it. I bet that's what's wrong."

"No," she said firmly. "Not you. That rope around its neck, that man with the spear, the look on that idiot woman's face — there, there's the hurt, five hundred years of it, five hundred frozen years of capture. Christ, Joe, let it sleep as long as it wants, let it heal." They were standing together, sometime in the night, looking down at the cat box, and she gripped Farrell's wrist hard.

"I knew right away," she said. "As soon as I saw it, I knew it wasn't just a religious allegory, a piece of a composition. I mean, yes, it was that too, but it was real, I could tell. Grandma could tell." NMC, awakened by their voices, looked up at them, yawning blissfully, round orange eyes glowing with secrets and self-satisfaction. Julie said, "There's nothing wrong with it that being out of that damn tapestry won't cure. Trust me, I was an art major."

"Shouldn't it be having something beside cat milk?" Farrell wondered. "I always figured unicorns lived on honey and — I don't know. Lilies, morning dew. Tule fog."

Julie shook her head against his shoulder. "Serenity," she said. Her voice was very low. "I think they live on serenity, and you can't get much more serene than that cat. Let's go to bed."

"Us? Us old guys?" Farrell was playing absently with her black hair, fanning his fingers out through it, tugging very gently. "You think we'll remember how it's done?"

"Don't get cute," she said, harshly enough to surprise them both. "Don't get cute, Farrell, don't get all charming. Just come to bed and hold me, and keep me company, and keep your mouth shut for a little while. You think you can manage that?"

"Yes, Jewel," Farrell said. "It doesn't use the litter box, did you notice?"

Julie dreamed of the unicorn that night. It had grown to full size and was trying to come into her bedroom, but couldn't quite fit through the door. She was frightened at first, when the great creature began to heave its prisoned shoulders, making the old house shudder around her until the roof rained shingles, and the stars came through. But in time it grew quiet, and other dreams tumbled between her and it as she slept with Farrell's arm over her, just as the unicorn slept with NMC.

In the morning, both of them late for work, unscrambling tangled clothing and exhuming a fossilized toothbrush of Farrell's ("All right, so I forgot to throw it out, so big deal!"), they nearly overlooked the unicorn altogether. It was standing — tapestry-size once again — at the foot of Julie's bed, regarding her out of eyes more violet than purple in the early light. She noticed for the first time that the pupils were horizontal, like those of a goat. NMC crouched in the doorway, switching her tail and calling plaintively for her strange foundling, but the unicorn had no heed for anyone but Julie. It lowered its head and stamped a mini-forefoot, and for all that the foot came down in a bright puddle of underwear it still made a sound like a bell ringing under the sea. Farrell and Julie, flurried as they were, stood very still.

The unicorn stamped a second time. Its eyes were growing brighter, passing from deep lavender through lilac, to blazing amethyst. Julie could not meet them. She whispered, "What is it? What do you want?"

Her only answer was a barely audible silver cry and the glint of the fierce little horn as the unicorn's ears slanted back against its head. Behind her Farrell, socks in hand, undershirt on backwards, murmured, "Critter wants to tell you something. Like Lassie."

"Shut up, Farrell," she snapped at him; then, to the unicorn, "Please, I don't understand. Please."

The unicorn raised its forefoot, as though about to stamp again. Instead, it trotted past the bed to the rickety little dressing table that Farrell had helped Julie put together very long ago, in another country. Barely the height of the lowest drawer, it looked imperiously back at them over its white shoulder before it turned, reared and stretched up as far as it could, like NMC setting herself for a luxurious, scarifying scratch. Farrell said, "The mirror."

"Shut up!" Julie said again; and then, "What?"

"The Cluny tapestries. *La Dame d la Licorne*. Unicorns like to look at themselves. Your hand mirror's up there." Julie stared at him for only a moment. She moved quickly to the dressing table, grabbed the mirror and crouched down close beside the unicorn. It shied briefly, but immediately after fell to gazing intently into the cracked, speckled glass with a curious air almost of puzzlement, as though it could not quite recognize itself. Julie wedged the mirror upright against the drawer-pull; then she rose and nudged Farrell, and the two of them hurriedly finished dressing, gulping boiled coffee while the unicorn remained where it was, seemingly oblivious of everything but its own image. When they left for work, Julie looked back anxiously, but Farrell said, "Let it be, don't worry, it'll stay where it is. I took Comparative Mythology, I know these things."

True to his prediction, the unicorn had not moved from the mirror when Julie came home late in the afternoon; and it was still in the same spot when Farrell arrived after the restaurant's closing. NMC was beside it, now pushing her head insistently against its side, now backing away to try one more forlorn mother-call, while the first kitten to make it into the wide world beyond the cat box was blissfully batting the tufted white tail back and forth. The tail's owner paid no slightest heed to either of them; but when Julie, out of curiosity, knelt and began to move the mirror away, the unicorn made a sound very like a kitten's hiss and struck at her fingers, barely missing. She stood up calmly, saying, "Well, I'm for banana cake, *Bringing Up Baby*, and having my feet rubbed. Later for Joseph Campbell." The motion was carried by acclamation.

The unicorn stayed by the mirror that night and all the next day, and the day after that. On the second day Julie came home to hear the sweet rubber-band sound of a lute in her apartment, and found Farrell sitting on the bed playing Dowland's "The Earl of Essex's Galliard." He looked up as she entered and told her cheerfully, "Nice acoustics you've got here. I've played halls that didn't sound half as good."

"That thing of yours about locks is going to get you busted one day," Julie said. The unicorn's eyes met hers in the hand mirror, but the creature did not stir. She asked, "Can you tell if it's listening at all?"

"Ears," Farrell said. "If the ears twitch even a bit, I try some more stuff by the same composer, or anyway the same century. Might not mean a thing, but it's all I've got to go by."

"Try Bach. Everything twitches to Bach."

Farrell snorted. "Forget it. Bourrees and sarabandes out the yingyang, and not a wiggle." Oddly, he sounded almost triumphant. "See, it's a conservative little soul, some ways — it won't respond to anything it wouldn't have heard in its own time. Which means, as far as I can make out, absolutely nothing past the fifteenth century. Binchois gets you one ear. Dufay — okay, both ears, I'm pretty sure it was both ears. Machaut — ears and a little tail action, we're really onto something now. Des Pres, jackpot — it actually turned and looked at me. Not for more than a moment, but that was some look. That was a look."

He sighed and scratched his head. "Not that any of this is any help to anybody. It's just that I'll never have another chance to play this old stuff for an informed critic, as you might say. Somebody who knows my music in a way I never will. Never mind. Just a thought."

Julie sat down beside him and put her arm around his shoulders. "Well, the hell with unicorns," she said. "What do unicorns know? Play Bach for me."

Whether Farrell's music had anything to do with it or not, they never knew; but morning found the unicorn across the room, balancing quite like a cat atop a seagoing uncle's old steamer trunk, peering down into the quiet street below. Farrell, already up and making breakfast, said, "It's looking for someone."

Julie was trying to move close to the unicorn without alarming it. Without looking at Farrell, she murmured, "By Gad, Holmes, you've done it again. Five hundred years out of its time, stranded in a cat box in California, what else would it be doing but meeting a friend for lunch? You make it look so easy, and I always feel so silly once you explain — "

"Cheap sarcasm doesn't become you, Tanikawa. Here, grab your tofu scramble while it's hot." He put the plate into the hand she extended backwards toward him. "Maybe it's trolling for virgins, what can I tell you? All I'm sure of, it looked in your mirror until it remembered itself, and now it knows what it wants to do. And too bad for us if we can't figure it out. I'm making the coffee with a little cinnamon, all right?"

The unicorn turned its head at their voices; then resumed its patient scrutiny of the dawn joggers, the commuters and the shabby, ambling pilgrims to nowhere. Julie said, slowly and precisely, "It was woven into that tapestry. It began in the tapestry — it can't know anyone who's not in the tapestry. Who could it be waiting for on East Redondo Street?"

Farrell had coffee for her, but no answer. They ate their breakfast in silence, looking at nothing but the unicorn, which looked at nothing but the street; until, as Farrell prepared to leave the apartment, it bounded lightly down from the old trunk and was at the door before him, purposeful and impatient. Julie came quickly, attempting for the first time to pick it up, but the unicorn backed against a bookcase and made the hissing-kitten sound again. Farrell said, "I wouldn't."

"Oh, I definitely would," she answered him between her teeth. "Because if it gets out that door, you're going to be the one chasing after it through Friday-morning traffic." The unicorn offered no resistance when she picked it up, though its neck was arched back like a coiled snake's and for a moment Julie felt the brilliant eyes burning her skin. She held it up so that it could see her own eyes, and spoke to it directly.

"I don't know what you want," she said. "I don't know what we could do to help you if we did know, as lost as you are. But it's my doing that you're here at all, so if you'll just be patient until Joe gets back, we'll take you outside, and maybe you can sort of show us. . ." Her voice trailed away, and she simply stared back into the unicorn's eyes. When Farrell cautiously opened the door, the unicorn paid no attention; nevertheless, he closed it to a crack behind him before he turned to say, "I have to handle lunch, but I can get off dinner. Just don't get careless. It's got something on its mind, that one."

With Farrell gone, she felt curiously excited and apprehensive at once, as though she were meeting another lover. She brought a chair to the window, placing it close to the steamer trunk. As soon as she sat down, NMC plumped into her lap, kittens abandoned, and settled down for some serious purring and shedding. Julie petted her absently, carefully avoiding glancing at the unicorn, or even thinking about it; instead she bent all her regard on what the unicorn must have seen from her window. She recognized the UPS driver, half a dozen local joggers — each sporting a flat-lipped grin of agony suggesting that their Walkman headphones were too tight — a policewoman whom she had met on birdwatching expeditions, and the Frozen-Yogurt Man. The Frozen-Yogurt Man wore a grimy naval officer's cap the year around, along with a flapping tweed sport jacket, sweat pants and calf-length rubber boots. He had a thin yellow-brown beard, like the stubble of a burned-over wheatfield, and had never been seen, as far as Julie knew, without a frozen-yogurt cone in at least one hand. Farrell said he favored plain vanilla in a sugar cone. "With M&Ms on top. Very California."

NMC raised an ear and opened an eye, and Julie turned her head to see the unicorn once again poised atop the steamer trunk, staring down at the Frozen-Yogurt Man with the soft hairs of its mane standing erect from nape to withers. (Did it pick that up from the cats? Julie wondered in some alarm.) "He's harmless," she said, feeling silly but needing to speak. "There must have been lots of people like him in your time. Only then there was a place for them, they had names, they fit the world somewhere. Mendicant friars, I guess. Hermits."

The unicorn leaped at the window. Julie had no more than a second's warning: the dainty head lowered only a trifle, the sleek miniature hindquarters seemed hardly to flex at all; but suddenly — so fast that she had no time even to register the explosion of the glass, the unicorn was nearly through. Blood raced down the white neck, tracing the curve of the straining belly.

Julie never remembered whether she cried out or not, never remembered moving. She was simply at the window with her hands surrounding the unicorn, pulling it back as gently as she possibly could, praying in silent desperation not to catch its throat on a fang of glass. Her hands were covered with blood — some of it hers — by the time the unicorn came free, but she saw quickly that its wounds were superficial, already coagulating and closing as she looked on. The unicorn's blood was as red as her own, but there was a strange golden shadow about it: a dark sparkling just under or beyond her eyes' understanding. She dabbed at it ineffectually with a paper towel, while the unicorn struggled in her grasp. Strangely, she could feel that it was not putting forth its entire strength; though whether from fear of hurting her or for some other reason, she could not say.

"All right," she said harshly. "All right. He's only the Frozen-Yogurt Man, for God's sake, but all right, I'll take you to him. I'll take you wherever you want — we won't wait for Joe, we'll just go out. Only you have to stay in my pocket. In my pocket, okay?"

The unicorn quieted slowly between her hands. She could not read the expression in the great, bruise-colored eyes, but it made no further attempt to escape when she set it down and began to patch the broken window with cardboard and packing tape. That done, she donned the St. Vincent de Paul duffel coat she wore all winter, and carefully deposited the unicorn in the wrist-deep right pocket. Then she pinned a note on the door for Farrell, pushed two kittens away from it with her foot, shut it, said aloud, "Okay, you got it," and went down into the street.

The sun was high and warm, but a chill breeze lurked in the shade of the old trees. Julie felt the unicorn move in her pocket, and looked down to see the narrow, delicate head out from under the flap. "Back in there," she said, amazed at her own firmness. "Five hundred, a thousand years — don't you know what happens by now? When people see you?" The unicorn retreated without protest.

She could see the Frozen-Yogurt Man's naval cap a block ahead, bobbing with his shuffling gait. There were a lot of bodies between them, and she increased her own pace, keeping a hand over her pocket as she slipped between strollers and dodged coffeehouse tables. Once, sidestepping a skateboarder, she tripped hard over a broken slab of sidewalk and stumbled to hands and knees, instinctively twisting her body to fall to the left. She was up in a moment, unhurt, hurrying on.

When she did catch up with the Frozen-Yogurt Man, and he turned his blindly benign gaze on her, she hesitated, completely uncertain of how to approach him. She had never spoken to him, nor even seen him close enough to notice that he was almost an albino, with coral eyes and pebbly skin literally the color of yogurt. She cupped her hand around the unicorn in her pocket, smiled and said, "Hi."

The Frozen-Yogurt Man said thoughtfully, as though they were picking up an interrupted conversation, "You think they know what they're doing?" His voice was loud and metallic, not quite connecting one word with another. It sounded to Julie like the synthesized voices that told her which buttons on her telephone to push.

"No," she answered without hesitation. "No, whatever you're talking about. I don't think anybody knows what they're doing anymore."

The Frozen-Yogurt Man interrupted her. "I think they do. I think they do. I think they do." Julie thought he might go on repeating the words forever; but she felt the stir against her side again, and the Frozen-Yogurt Man's flat pink eyes shifted and widened. "What's that?" he demanded shrilly. "What's that watching me?"

The unicorn was halfway out of her coat pocket, front legs flailing as it yearned toward the Frozen-Yogurt Man.

Only the reluctance of passersby to make eye contact with either him or Julie spared the creature from notice. She grabbed it with both hands, forcing it back, telling it in a frantic hiss, "Stay there, you stay, he isn't the one! I don't know whom you're looking for, but it's not him." But the unicorn thrashed in the folds of cloth as though it were drowning.

The Frozen-Yogurt Man was backing away, his hands out, his face melting. Ever afterward, glimpsing him across the street, Julie felt chillingly guilty for having seen him so. In a phlegmy whisper he said, "Oh, no — oh, no, no, you don't put that thing on me. No, I been watching you all the time, you get away, you get away from me with that thing. You people, you put that chip behind my ear, you put them radio mice in my stomach you get away, you don't put nothing more on me, you done me enough." He was screaming now, and the officer's cap was tipping forward, revealing a scarred scalp the color of the sidewalk. "You done me enough! You done me enough!"

Julie fled. She managed at first to keep herself under control, easing away sedately enough through the scattering of mildly curious spectators; it was only when she was well down the block and could still hear the Frozen-Yogurt Man's terrified wailing that she began to run. Under the hand that she still kept in her pocket, the unicorn seemed to have grown calm again, but its heart was beating in tumultuous rhythm with her own. She ran on until she came to a bus stop and collapsed on the bench there, gasping for breath, rocking back and forth, weeping dryly for the Frozen-Yogurt Man.

She came back to herself only when she felt the touch of a cool, soft nose just under her right ear. Keeping her head turned away, she said hoarsely, "Just let me sit here a minute, all right? I did what you wanted. I'm sorry it didn't work out. You get back down before somebody sees you." A warm breath stirred the hairs on Julie's arms, and she raised her head to meet the hopeful brown eyes and all-purpose grin of a young golden retriever. The dog was looking brightly back and forth between her and the unicorn, wagging its entire body from the ears on down, back feet dancing eagerly. The unicorn leaned precariously from Julie's pocket to touch noses with it.

"No one's ever going to believe you," Julie said to the dog. The golden retriever listened attentively, waited a moment to make certain she had no more to confide, and then gravely licked the unicorn's head, the great red tongue almost wrapping it round. NMC's incessant grooming had plainly not prepared the unicorn for anything like this; it sneezed and took refuge in the depths of the pocket. Julie said, "Not a living soul."

The dog's owner appeared then, apologizing and grabbing its dangling leash to lead it away. It looked back, whining, and its master had to drag it all the way to the corner. Julie still huddled and rocked on the bus stop bench, but when the unicorn put its head out again she was laughing thinly. She ran a forefinger down its mane, and then laid two fingers gently against the wary, pulsing neck. She said, "Burnouts. Is that it? You're looking for one of our famous Avicenna loonies, none with less than a master's, each with a direct line to Mars, Atlantis, Lemuria, Graceland or Mount Shasta? Is that it?" For the first time, the unicorn pushed its head hard into her hand, as NMC would do. The horn pricked her palm lightly.

For the next three hours, she made her way from the downtown streets to the university's red-tiled enclave, and back again, with small side excursions into doorways, subway stations, even parking lots. She developed a peculiar cramp in her neck from snapping frequent glances at her pocket to be sure that the unicorn was staying out of sight. Whenever it indicated interest in a wild red gaze, storks'-nest hair, a shopping cart crammed with green plastic bags, or a droning monologue concerning Jesus, AIDS, and the Kennedys, she trudged doggedly after one more street apostle to open one more conversation with the moon. Once the unicorn showed itself, the result was always the same.

"It likes beards," she told Farrell late that night, as he patiently massaged her feet. "Bushy beards — the wilder and filthier, the better. Hair, too, especially that pattern baldness tonsure look. Sandals, yes, definitely — it doesn't like boots or sneakers at all, and it can't make up its mind about Birkenstocks. Prefers blankets and serapes to coats, dark hair to light, older to younger, the silent ones to the walking sound trucks — men to women, absolutely. Won't even stick its head out for a woman."

"It's hard to blame the poor thing," Farrell mused. "For a unicorn, men would be a bunch of big, stupid guys with swords and whatnot. Women are betrayal, every time, simple as that. It wasn't Gloria Steinem who wove that tapestry." He squeezed toes gently with one hand, a bruised heel with the other. "What did they do when they actually saw it?"

The unicorn glanced at them over the edge of the cat box, where its visit had been cause for an orgy of squeaking, purring and teething. Julie said, "What do you think? It was bad. It got pretty damn awful. Some of them fell down on their knees and started laughing and crying and praying their heads off. There were a couple who just sort of crooned and moaned to it — and I told you about the poor Frozen-Yogurt Man — and then there was one guy who tried to grab it away and run off with it. But it wasn't having that, and it jabbed him really hard. Nobody noticed, thank God." She laughed wearily, presenting her other foot for treatment. "The rest — oh, I'd say they should be halfway to Portland by now. Screaming all the way."

Farrell grunted thoughtfully, but asked no more questions until Julie was in bed and he was sitting across the room playing her favorite Campion lute song. She was nearly asleep when his voice bumbled slowly against her half-dream like a fly at a window. "It can't know anyone who's not in the tapestry. There's the answer. There it is."

"There it is," she echoed him, barely hearing her own words. Farrell put down the lute and came to her, sitting on the bed to grip her shoulder.

"Jewel, listen, wake up and listen to me! It's trying to find someone who was in that tapestry with it — we even know what he looks like, more or less. An old guy, ragged and dirty, big beard, sandals — some kind of monk, most likely. Though what a unicorn would be doing anywhere near your average monk is more than I can figure. Are you awake, Jewel?"

"Yes," she mumbled. "No. Wasn't anybody else. Sleep." Somewhere very far away Farrell said, "We didn't see anybody else." Julie felt the bed sway as he stood up. "Tomorrow night," he said. "Tomorrow's Saturday, they stay open later on Saturdays. You sleep, I'll call you." She drifted off in confidence that he would lock the door carefully behind him, even without a key.

A temporary word-processing job, in company with a deadline for a set of views of diseased kidneys, filled up most of the next day for her. She was still weary, vaguely depressed, and grateful when she returned home to find the unicorn thoroughly occupied in playing on the studio floor with three of NMC's kittens. The game appeared to involve a good deal of stiff-legged pouncing, an equal amount of spinning and side-slipping on the part of the unicorn, all leading to a grand climax in which the kittens tumbled furiously over one another while the unicorn looked on, forgotten until the next round. They never came close to laying a paw on their swift littermate, and the unicorn in turn treated them with effortless care. Julie watched for a long time, until the kittens abruptly fell asleep.

"I guess that's what being immortal is like," she said aloud. The unicorn looked back at her, its eyes gone almost black. Julie said, "One minute they're romping around with you — the next, they're sleeping. Right in the middle of the game. We're all kittens to you."

The unicorn did a strange thing then. It came to her and indicated with an imperious motion of its head that it wanted to be picked up. Julie bent down to lift it, and it stepped off her joined palms into her lap, where — after pawing gently for a moment, like a dog settling in for the night — it folded its long legs and put its head down. Julie's heart hiccupped absurdly in her breast.

"I'm not a virgin," she said. "But you know that." The unicorn closed its eyes.

Neither of them had moved when Farrell arrived, looking distinctly irritated and harassed. "I left Gracie to finish up," he said. "Gracie. If I still have my job tomorrow, it'll be more of a miracle than any mythical beast. Let's go."

In the van, with the unicorn once again curled deep in Julie's pocket, Farrell said, "What we have to do is, we have to take a look at the tapestry again. A good long look this time."

"It's not going back there. I told you that." She closed her hand lightly around the unicorn, barely touching it, more for her own heartening than its reassurance. "Joe, if that's what you're planning —"

Farrell grinned at her through the timeless fast-food twilight of Madame Schumann-Heink. "No wonder you're in such good shape, all that jumping to conclusions. Listen, there has to be some other figure in that smudgy thing, someone we didn't see before. Our little friend has a friend."

Julie considered briefly, then shook her head. "No. No way. There was the knight, the squire, and that woman. That's all, I'm sure of it."

"Um," Farrell said. "Now, me, I'm never entirely sure of anything.

You've probably noticed, over the years. Come on, Madame, you can do it." He dropped the van into first gear and gunned it savagely up a steep, narrow street. "We didn't see the fourth figure because we weren't looking for it. But it's there, it has to be. This isn't Comparative Mythology, Jewel, this is me."

Madame Schumann-Heink actually gained the top of the hill without stalling, and Farrell rewarded such valor by letting the old van free-wheel down the other side. Julie said slowly, "And if it is there? What happens then?"

"No idea. The usual. Play it by ear and trust we'll know the right thing to do. You will, anyway. You always know the right thing to do, Tanikawa."

The casual words startled her so deeply that she actually covered her mouth for a moment: a classic Japanese mannerism she had left behind in her Seattle childhood.

"You never told me that before. Twenty years, and you never said anything, like that to me." Farrell was crooning placatingly to Madame Schumann-Heink's brake shoes, and did not answer. Julie said, "Even if I did always know, which I don't, I don't always do it. Not even usually. Hardly ever, the way I feel right now."

Farrell let the van coast to a stop under a traffic light before he turned to her. His voice was low enough that she had to bend close to hear him. "All I know," he said, "there are two of us girls in this heap, and one of us had a unicorn sleeping in her lap a little while back. You work it out." He cozened Madame Schumann-Heink back into gear, and they lurched on toward the Bigby Museum.

A different guard this time: trimmer, younger, far less inclined to speculative conversation, and even less likely to overlook dubious goings-on around the exhibits.

Fortunately, there was also a university-sponsored lecture going on: it appeared to be the official word on the Brueghels, and had drawn a decent house for a Saturday night. Under his breath, Farrell said, "We split up. You go that way, I'll ease around by the Spanish stuff. Take your time."

Julie took him at his word, moving slowly through the crowd and pausing occasionally for brief murmured conversations with academic acquaintances. Once she plainly took exception to the speaker's comments regarding Brueghel's artistic debt to his father-in-law, and Farrell, watching from across the room, fully expected her to interrupt the lecture with a discourse of her own. But she resisted temptation; they met, as planned, by the three tapestries, out of the guard's line of sight, and with only a single bored-looking browser anywhere near them. Julie held Farrell's hand tightly as they turned to study the middle tapestry.

Nothing had changed. The knight and squire still prodded a void toward their pale lady, who went on leaning forward to drape her wreath around captive space. Julie imagined a bleak recognition in their eyes of knotted thread that had not been there before, but she felt foolish about that and said nothing to Farrell. Silently the two of them divided the tapestry into fields of survey, as they had done with the gallery itself when the unicorn first escaped. Julie took the foreground, scanning the ornamental garden framing the three human figures for one more face, likely dirty and bearded, perhaps by now so faded as to merge completely with the faded leaves and shadows. She was on her third futile sweep over the scene when she heard Farrell's soft hiss beside her.

"Yes!" he whispered. "Got you, you godly little recluse, you. I knew you had to be in there!" He grabbed Julie's hand and drew it straight up to the vegetable-looking forest surrounding the distant castle. "Right there, peeping coyly out like Julia's feet, you can't miss him."

But she could, and she did, for a maddening while; until Farrell made her focus on a tiny shape, a gray-white bulge at the base of one of the trees. Nose hard against the glass, she began at last to see it clearly: all robe and beard, mostly, but stitched with enough maniacal medieval detail to suggest a bald head, intense black eyes and a wondering expression. Farrell said proudly, "Your basic resident hermit. Absolutely required, no self-respecting feudal estate complete without one. There's our boy."

It seemed to Julie that the lady and the two men were straining their embroidered necks to turn toward the castle and the solitary form they had forgotten for five centuries. "Him?" she said. "He's the one?"

"Hold our friend up to see him. Watch what happens." For a while, afterward, she tried to forget how grudgingly she had reached into her coat pocket and slowly brought her cupped hand up again, into the light. Farrell shifted position, moving close on her right to block any possible glimpse of the unicorn. It posed on Julie's palm, head high, three legs splayed slightly for balance, and one forefoot proudly curled (*exactly like every unicorn I ever drew when I was young*, she thought). She looked around quickly — half afraid of being observed, half wishing it — and raised her hand to bring the unicorn level with the dim little figure of the hermit.

Three things happened then. The unicorn uttered a harsh, achingly plain cry of recognition and longing, momentarily silencing the Brueghel lecturer around the corner. At the same time, a different sound, low and disquieting, like a sleeper's teeth grinding together, seemed to come either from the frame enclosing the tapestry or the glass over it. The third occurrence was that something she could not see, nor ever after describe to Farrell, gripped Julie's right wrist so strongly that she cried out herself and almost dropped the unicorn to the gallery floor. She braced it with her free hand as it scrambled for purchase, the carpet-tack horn glowing like abalone shell.

"What is it, what's the matter?" Farrell demanded. He made clumsily to hold her, but she shook him away. Whatever had her wrist tightened its clamp, feeling nothing at all like a human hand, but rather as though the air itself were turning to stone — as though one part of her were being buried while the rest stood helplessly by. Her fingers could yet move, enough to hold the unicorn safe; but there was no resisting the force that was pushing her arm back down toward the tapestry foreground, back to the knight and the squire, the mincing damsel and the strangling garden. They want it. It is theirs. Give it to them. They want it.

"Fat fucking chance, buster," she said loudly. Her right hand was almost numb, but she felt the unicorn rearing in her palm, felt its rage shock through her stone arm, and watched from very far away as the bright horn touched the tapestry frame.

Almost silently, the glass shattered. There was only one small hole at first, popping into view just above the squire's lumpy face; then the cracks went spidering across the entire surface, making a tiny scratching sound, like mice in the walls. One by one, quite deliberately, the pieces of glass began to fall out of the frame, to splinter again on the hardwood floor.

With the first fragment, Julie's arm was her own once more, freezing cold and barely controllable, but free. She lurched forward, off-balance, and might easily have shoved the unicorn back into the garden after all. But Farrell caught her, steadying her hand as she raised it to the shelter of the forest and the face under the trees.

The unicorn turned its head. Julie caught the brilliant purple glance out of the air and tucked it away in herself, to keep for later. She could hear voices approaching now, and quick, officious footsteps that didn't sound like those of an art historian. As briskly as she might have shooed one of NMC's kittens from underfoot, she said, in the language that sounded like Japanese, "Go on, then, go. Go home."

She never actually saw the unicorn flow from her hand into the tapestry. Whenever she tried to make herself recall the moment, memory dutifully producing a rainbow flash or a melting movie-dissolve passage between worlds, irritable honesty told memory to put a sock in it. There was never anything more than herself standing in a lot of broken glass for the second time in two days, with a faint chill in her right arm, hearing Farrell's eloquently indignant voice denying to guards, docents and lecturers alike that either of them had laid a hand on this third-rate Belgian throw rug. He was still expounding a theory involving cool recycled air on the outside of the glass and warm condensation within as they were escorted all the way to the parking lot. When Julie praised his passionate inventiveness, he only growled, "Maybe that's the way it really was. How do I know?"

But she knew without asking that he had seen what she had seen: the pale shadow peering back at them from its sanctuary in the wood, and the opaline glimmer of a horn under the hermit's hand. Knight, lady and squire — one another's prisoners now, eternally — remained exactly where they were.

That night neither Farrell nor Julie slept at all. They lay silently close, peacefully wide-awake, companionably solitary, listening to her beloved Black-Forest-tourist-trash cuckoo clock strike the hours. In the morning Farrell said it was because NMC had carried on so, roaming the apartment endlessly in search of her lost nursling. But Julie answered, "We didn't need to sleep. We needed to be quiet and tell ourselves what happened to us. To hear the story."

Farrell was staring blankly into the open refrigerator, as he had been for some time. "I'm still not sure what happened. I get right up to the place where you lifted it up so it could see its little hermit buddy, and then your arm. . . I can't ever figure that part. What the hell was it that had hold of you?"

"I don't see how we'll ever know," she said. "It could have been them, those three — some force they were able to put out together that almost made me put the unicorn back with them, in the garden." She shivered briefly, then slipped past him to take out the eggs, milk and smoked salmon he had vaguely been seeking, and close the refrigerator door.

Farrell shook his head slowly. "They weren't real. Not like the unicorn. Even your grandmother couldn't have brought one of them to life on this side. Colored thread, that's all they were. The hermit, the monk, whatever — I don't know, Jewel."

"I don't know either," she said. "Listen. Listen, I'll tell you what I think I think. Maybe whoever wove that tapestry meant to trap a unicorn, meant to keep it penned up there forever. Not a wicked wizard, nothing like that, just the weaver, the artist. It's the way we are, we all want to paint or write or play something so for once it'll stay painted, stay played, stay put, so it'll still be alive for us tomorrow, next week, always. Mostly it dies in the night — but now and then, now and then, somebody gets it right. And when you get it right, then it's real. Even if it doesn't exist, like a unicorn, if you get it really right. . ."

She let the last words trail away. Farrell said, "Garlic. I bet you don't have any garlic, you never do." He opened the refrigerator again and rummaged, saying over his shoulder, "So you think it was the weaver himself, herself, grabbing you, from back there in the fifteenth century? Wanting you to put things back the way you found them, the way he had it — the right way?"

"Maybe." Julie rubbed her arm unconsciously, though the coldness was long since gone. "Maybe. Too bad for him. Right isn't absolutely everything."

"Garlic is," Farrell said from the depths of the vegetable bin. Emerging in triumph, brandishing a handful of withered-looking cloves, he added, "That's my Jewel. Priorities on straight, and a strong but highly negotiable sense of morality. The thing I've always loved about you, all these years."

Neither of them spoke for some while. Farrell peeled garlic and broke eggs into a bowl, and Julie fed NMC. The omelets were almost done before she said, "We might manage to put up with each other a bit longer than usual this time. Us old guys. I mean, I've signed a lease on this place, I can't go anywhere."

"Hand me the cayenne," Farrell said. "Madame Schumann-Heink's can still manage the Bay Bridge these days, but I don't think I'd try her over the Golden Gate. Your house and the restaurant, that's about her limit."

"You'd probably have to go a bit light on the garlic. Only a bit, that's all. And I still don't like people around when I'm working. And I still read in the bathroom."

Farrell smiled at her then, brushing gray hair out of his eyes. "That's all right, there's always the litter box. Just don't you go marrying any Brians. Definitely no Brians."

"Fair enough," she said. "Think of it — you could have a real key, and not have to pick the lock every time. Hold still, there's egg on your forehead." The omelets got burned.

THE NAGA

AUTHOR'S NOTE

The following tale is a fragment of a recently discovered first-century Roman manuscript, tentatively ascribed to Caius Plinius Secundus, known as Pliny the Elder. It appears to be an addendum to his great *Encyclopedia of Natural History*, and to have been written shortly before his death in 79 A.D., in the eruption of Mount Vesuvius. How it fell into the present writer's hands is another story entirely, and is no one's business but his own.

— *P.S.B.*

Let us begin with a creature of which report has reached us only from those half-mythical lands beyond the Indus, where dwell many dragons and unicorns as well. The naga is described by such traders as travel between India and the Roman provinces of Mesopotamia as being a great serpent with seven heads, like the beast known to us as the hydra. Leaving aside the history of Hercules's conquest of the Lernaean Hydra, authorities have related numerous encounters with these animals off the coasts of Greece and Britain. The hydra has between seven and ten heads, like dogs' heads: these are generally depicted as growing at the ends of prodigiously muscular necks or arms, and they do not devour the prey they seize but drag it to a central head, much larger, which then tears it apart with a beak like that of a monstrous African parrot. Further, it is said that these heads and necks, cut in two, do grow again: on the instant, according to the Greek writers, but their capacity both for lying and credulity surpasses all bounds that one might reasonably impose on other peoples. Nevertheless, of the hydra's actual existence there can be little doubt — I have myself spoken with sailors who had lost comrades to the voracity of these beasts, and who, in vengeance, would boil one alive and devour it themselves whenever they should capture one. I am advised that the taste of the hydra is quite similar to that of the boots of which soldiers often make soup in desert extremities. The flavor is not easily forgotten.

But the naga is plainly another nature of being from the hydra, whatever their superficial resemblances. Such accounts as I have received indicate that the folk of India and the lands beyond generally revere this creature, indeed considering it almost as a god, yet at the same time somehow lower than the human. The contradictions do not end here, for though the bite of the naga is reputedly poisonous to all that lives, only certain individuals are regarded as physically dangerous to man. (Indeed, there appears to be no agreement among my sources as to the usual prey of the naga: several authorities even suggest that the beast does not eat at all, but lives on the milk of the wild elephant, which it herds and protects as we do cattle.) Water is the nagas' element: they are believed to have the power to bring rain, or to withhold it, and consequently must be propitiated with sacrifices and other offerings, and treated with constant respect. As do dragons here, they guard great hoards of gold in deep lairs; but much unlike the dragons we know, the nagas reportedly construct underground palaces of immense richness and beauty, dwelling there in the manner of kings and queens in this world. Yet it is said that they are often restless, pining for something they cannot have, and then they leave their mansions and stir forth into the rivers and brooks of India. The philosophers of that region say that they are seeking enlightenment — there are sects in Rome who would assure us that they hunger for a human soul. I have no opinion in this matter.

It may be of some interest to those who have served the Emperor in Britain to know that a creature similar to the naga is rumored to exist in the far northern marches of that island, where it is worshipped as a bringer of fertility, perhaps because it sleeps out the winter months underground, emerging on the first day of spring. But whether or not these serpents amass treasure in the same manner as the nagas, and as to how many heads they have, I know not.

All nagas are said to possess a priceless jewel, located either in the forehead or the throat, which is the source of their great power. They are, like the elephant, of a religious and even reverential nature, frequently keeping up shrines to the gods of India and making rich offerings of the same sort as they themselves receive. In addition, there are accounts of naga kings presenting their bodies as couches for the gods, spreading their hoods to keep off the rain and sun. Whether or not these tales are true, that they should be credited at all certainly indicates the regard in which the nagas are held in these lands.

A further puzzling contradiction concerning the naga is the general understanding that the female serpent — referred to as a nagini — is capable of assuming the human shape, while this is not so for the male of the species. In this counterfeit form, the nagini is frequently of remarkable beauty, and it is said that there are royal families who trace their descent from the marriage of a mortal prince with a nagini. Regarding this matter, the following tale was related directly to me by a trader in silks and dyestuffs who has traveled widely both in India and in the neighboring realm to the east, called by its folk Kambuja. I will repeat it in the manner of his telling, as well as I am able.

> In Kambuja, a little way from the palace of the kings, there stands to this day a tower sheathed completely in gold, as is often the style of royalty in those parts. This tower was built very long ago by a young king, as soon as he rose to power, to serve as apartments for himself and his queen when he should marry. But in the arrogance of his youth, he was impatient and impossible to please: this maiden was too plain, that one too dull; this one pretty enough but too quick-tongued, and this other was an unsuitable match for family reasons, and smelled of dried fish to boot. Consequently, his first youth passed in the solitude of majesty, which — as I am often advised — can surely be no substitute for the companionship and loving wisdom of a true wife, whether queen or bondservant. And the king was ever more lonely, though he would not say so, and ill-tempered because of this; and while he was not cruel or capricious in his ways,

still he ruled in a listless fashion, doing little of evil and no good, having no heart for either. And the golden tower went untenanted, year on year, save for spiders and small owls raising their own families in the topmost spire.

Now (said the trader), this king was much in the habit of walking disguised among his people in the warm twilight of the streets and the marketplace. He fancied that he gained some knowledge of their true daily lives thereby, which was not at all so: first, because there was no least urchin but recognized him on sight, however wearily cunning his incognito; and secondly, because he had no real desire for such understanding. Nevertheless, he kept his custom faithfully enough, and one evening a beggar woman with a dirty and ignorant face approached him on his meanderings and inquired in a vulgar dialect, "Your pardon, master potter —" (for so he was dressed) "— but what is the nature of that shiny thing there?" And she pointed toward the golden tower that the king had designed for his happiness so long ago.

Now the king was apparently not without humor, albeit of a bleak and comfortless sort. He replied courteously to the beggar woman, saying, "That is a museum consecrated to the memory of one who never lived, and I am no potter but its very guardian. Would you care to satisfy your curiosity? for we welcome visitors, the tower and I" The beggar woman assented readily, and the king took her by the hand and led her, first through the gardens that he had planted with his own hands, and then through the great shining door to which he always carried the key, though it had never turned in the lock until that day.

From room to room and spire to spire the king led the beggar woman, conversing with her all the time in grave mockery of his own past dreams. "Here is where he would have dined, this man who never was, and in this room he would have sat with his wife and his friends to hear musicians play. And this place was to have been for his wife's women, and this for children to sleep as though the unborn could father children." But when they came to the royal bedchamber, the king drew back from the door and would not go in, but said harshly, "There are serpents here, and plague, come away."

But the beggar woman stepped boldly past him and into the bedchamber with the air of one who has been long away from a place, yet remembers it well. The king called to her in anger, and when she turned he saw (said the trader) that she was no creeping beggar but a great queen, clad in robes and jewels far richer than any he possessed himself. And she said to him, "I am a nagini, come from my palace and my estates far under the earth, for love and pity of you. From this evening forward, neither you nor I shall sleep elsewhere but in this tower ever again." And the king embraced her, for she was of such royal loveliness that he could do no other; and besides, he had been much alone.

Presently, some degree of order having returned to their joy, the king began to speak of their wedding, of festivals to last for months, and of how they would rule and keep their court together. But the nagini said, "Beloved, we are twice wed already: once when I first saw your face, and again when we first held one another in our arms. As for counselors and armies and decrees, that is all your daytime world and none of mine. My own realm, my own folk, need my care and governance as much as yours need you. But in our night world we will care for each other here, and how can our dutiful days but be happy, with night always to come?"

The king was not content with this, for he wished to present his people with their long-awaited queen, and to have her by his side at every moment of every day. He said to her, "I can see that we shall come to no good end. You will tire of journeying constantly between two worlds and forget me for some naga lord, compared to whom I shall seem as a sweeper, a date-seller. And I, in my sorrow, will turn to a street-singer, a common courtesan, or — worse — a woman of the court, and be more lonely and more strange than ever for having loved you. Is this the gift that you have come all this long way to bring me?"

At that, the nagini's long, beautiful eyes flashed, and she caught the king by his wrists, saying, "Never speak to me of jealousy and betrayal, even in jest. My folk are faithful through all their lives — can you say the same of yours? And I will tell you this, my own lord, my one — should night ever come to this tower and not bring you with it, it will not be morning before a terrible catastrophe befalls your kingdom. If even once you fail to meet me here, nothing will save Kambuja from my wrath. That is how we are, we nagas."

"And if you do not come to me each night," said the king simply, "I shall die." Then the nagini's eyes filled with tears, and she put her arms about him, saying, 'Why do we vex each other with talk of what will never happen? We are home together at last, my friend, my husband." And of their happiness in the golden tower there is no further need to speak, save to add that the spiders and serpents and owls were all gone from there by morning.

Thus it was that the king of Kambuja took a nagini as his queen, even though she came to him only in darkness, and only in the golden tower.

He told no one of this, as she bade him; but since he abandoned all matters of state, all show and ceremony, as soon as the sun set, to hurry alone to the tower, rumors that he met a woman there every night spread swiftly through all the country. The curious followed him as closely and as far as they dared; and there were even those who waited all night outside the tower in hopes of spying out the king's secret mistress as she came and went. But none ever saw even the shadow of the nagini — only the king, walking slowly back into the day, calm and pensive, his face shining with the last light of the moon.

In time, however, such gossip and fascination gave way to wonder at the change in the king. For he ruled more and more with a passionate awareness of his people's real existence, as though he had awakened to see them for the first time, in all their human innocence and wickedness and suffering. From caring about nothing but his own bitter loneliness, he now began to work at bettering their lot as intensely as they themselves worked merely to survive. There was no one in the realm who could not see and speak freely to him: no condemned criminal, overtaxed merchant, beaten servant or daughter sold into marriage who could not appeal and be heard. Such zealous concern bewildered many who were accustomed to other sorts of rulers, and a half-mocking saying grew up in the land: "By night we have a queen, but by day we have at least five kings." Yet slowly his people came to return their king's love, if not to comprehend it, and it came also to be said that if justice existed nowhere else in the entire universe, still it had been invented in Kambuja.

The reason for this change, as the king himself well knew, was twofold: first, that he was happy for the first time in his life and wished to see others happy; second, that it seemed to him that the harder he worked, the faster the day sped its course, carrying him to nightfall and his nagini queen. In its turn, as she had told him, the joy that he took in their love, made even their hours apart joyous by reflection, as the sun, long since set, yet brightens our nights through the good offices of the moon. So it is that one learns to treasure, without confusing them, day and night and twilight alike, with all that they contain.

The years passed swiftly, being made up of days and nights as they are. The king never spent a night away from the golden tower — which meant, among many other things, that during his reign Kambuja never went to war — and the nagini was always there when he arrived to greet him by the secret name that the priests had given him as a child, the name that no one else knew. In return she had told him her naga name (and laughed fondly at his attempts to speak it correctly), but she refused ever to let him see her in her true shape, as she went among her own folk. "What I am with you is what I am most truly," she said to him (according to the sworn word of my trader). "We nagas are forever passing between water and earth, earth and air, between one form and another, one world and another, this desire and that, this dream and that. Here in our tower I am as you know me, neither more nor less; and what shape you put on when you sit and give judgment on life and death, I do not ask to see. Here we are both as free as though you were not a king and I were not a naga. Let it remain so, my dear one."

The king answered, "It shall be as you say, but you should know that there are many who whisper that their night queen is indeed a naga. The land has grown too bounteous, the rainfall is too perfect, too reliable — who but a naga could command such precise good fortune? Most of my people have believed for years that you are the true ruler of Kambuja, whatever else you may be. In truth, I find it hard to disagree with them."

"I have never told you how to govern your country," the nagini answered him. "You needed no instruction from me to be a king."

"You think not?" he asked her then. "But I was no king at all until you came to me, and my people know that as well as I. Perhaps you never taught me to build a road or a granary, to devise a just tax or keep my land's borders free of enemies, but without you I would never have cared that I could do such things. Once Kambuja was only to be endured because it contained our golden tower; now, by little and little, the tower has grown to take in all Kambuja, and all my people have come inside with us, precious as ourselves. This is your doing, and this is why you rule here, by day as well as night."

At times he would say to her, "Long ago, when I told you that I would die if you ever failed to meet me here, your face changed and I knew that I had spoken more truth than I meant. I know now — so wise has loving made me — that one night you will not come, and I will die indeed, and for that I care nothing. I have known you. I have lived." But the nagini would never let him speak further, weeping and promising him that such a night would never be, and then the king would comfort her until morning. So they were together, and the years passed.

The king grew old with the nagini as he had been young with her, joyously and without fear. But those most near to him grew old too, and died or retired from the court, and there emerged a rabble of young soldiers and courtiers who grumbled loudly that the king had provided no heir to the throne, and that the realm would be torn to pieces by his squabbling cousins at his death. They complained further that he was in such thrall to his nagini, or his sorceress, or his leopard-woman (for the belief in such shape-changers is a common one in Kambuja) that he took little care for the glory and renown of the kingdom, so that Kambuja had become a byword for well-fed timidity among other nations. And if none of this was true, still it is well-known that long tranquility makes many restless, ready to follow anyone who promises tumultuous change for its own sake. It has happened so even in Rome.

Several attempted to warn the king that such was the case at his court, but he paid no heed, preferring to believe that all around him were as serene as he. Thus, when a drowsy noon hour abruptly shattered into blood and shouting and the clanging of swords, and even when he found himself with his back to his own throne-room door, fighting for his life, the king was not prepared. If the best third of his army, made up of his strongest veterans, had not remained loyal, the battle would have been over in those first few minutes, and there would be no more than this to my trader's story. But the king's forces held on doggedly, and then rallied, and by mid-afternoon were on the attack; so that as the sun began to set the insurrection had dwindled to a few pockets of a few desperate rebels who fought like madmen, knowing that no surrender would be accepted. It was in combat with one such that the king of Kambuja received his mortal wound.

He did not know that it was mortal. He knew only that night was falling, and that there were yet men standing between him and the golden tower, men who had screamed all afternoon that they would kill him first and then his leopard-woman, his serpent-woman, the monster who had for so long rotted the fiber of the realm. So he struck them down with all his remaining strength, and then he turned, half-naked, covered with blood, and limped away from battle toward the tower. If men barred his way, he killed them; but he fell often, and each time he was slower to rise, which made him angry. The tower seemed to grow no closer and he knew that he should be with his nagini by now.

He would never have reached the tower, but for the valor of a very young officer, far younger than boys in Rome have ever been permitted to enter the Emperor's service. This boy's commander, whose personal charge was the safety of the king, had been slain early in the rebellion, and the boy had appointed himself the king's shield in his stead, following the king through all the dusty turmoil of battle and ever fighting at his side or his back. Now he ran forward to raise the king and support him, all but carrying him toward that distant door through which he had jestingly led a beggar woman so long ago. None of either side came near them as they struggled through the twilight: none dared.

By the time they at last attained the tower door, the boy knew that the king was dying. He had no strength to turn the key in the lock, nor could he even speak, save with his eyes, to order the boy to do it; yet once they were within, he pulled himself to his feet and climbed the stairs like any eager young man hastening to his beloved. The boy trailed behind, frightened of this place of his parents' nursery stories, this high darkness rustling with demon queens. Yet care for his king overcame all such terrors, and he was once again at the old man's side when they stood on the bedchamber threshold with the door swinging open before them.

The nagini was not there. The boy hurried to light the torches on the walls, and saw that the chamber was barren of everything but shadows; shadows and the least, least smell of jasmine and sandalwood. Behind him, the king said clearly, "She has not come." The boy was not quick enough to catch him when he fell. His eyes were open when the boy lifted him in his arms and he pointed toward the bed without speaking. When the boy had set him there, and bound his many wounds as best he could, the king beckoned him close and whispered, "Watch the night. Watch with me." It was no plea, but a command.

So the boy sat all through the night on the great bed where the king and queen of Kambuja had slept in happiness for so long, and he never knew when the king died. He fought to stay awake as hard as he had fought the king's enemies that day, but he was weary and wounded himself, and he dozed and woke and dozed again. The last time he roused, it was because all the torches had gone out at once, with a sound like a ship's sails cracking in the breeze, and because he heard another sound, heavy and slow, some cold, rough burden being dragged over cold stone. In the last moonlight he saw her: the vast body filling the room like greenish-black smoke, the seven cobra heads swaying as one, and a flickering about her, as though she were shimmering between two worlds at a speed his eyes could not understand. She was close enough to the bed for him to see that she too bore fresh, bleeding wounds (he said later that her blood was as bright as the sun, and hurt his eyes.) When he hurled himself away, rolling and scrambling into a corner, the nagini never looked at him. She bowed her seven heads over the king as he lay, and her burning blood fell and mingled with his blood.

"My people tried to keep me from you," she said. The boy could not tell whether all the heads spoke; or only one; he said that her voice was full of other voices, like a chord of music. The nagini said, "They told me that today was the day appointed for your death, fixed in the atoms of the universe since the beginning of time, and so it was, and I have always known this, as you knew. But I could not turn away and let it be so, fated or not, and I fought them and came here. He who hides in the shadows will sing that you and I never once failed each other, neither in life nor in death."

Then she called the king by a name that the boy did not recognize, and she took him up onto the coils of her body, as the folk of these parts believe that a naga named Muchalinda supports this world and those to come. Nor did she leave the bedchamber by the door, but passed slowly into darkness, vanishing with no more trace than the scent of jasmine and sandalwood, and the fading music of all her voices. And what became of her, and of the remains of the king of Kambuja, is not known.

Now I find this story open to some question — there is more evidence to be offered for the existence of nagas than proof positive that they do not exist; but of their commerce with men, much may safely be doubted. But I set it down even so, in honor of that boy who waited until sunrise in that silent golden tower before he dared walk out among the clamor of kites and the moans of the grieving to tell the people of Kambuja that their king was dead and gone. One of his descendants it was — or so he swore — who told me the tale.

And if there is any sort of message or metaphor in it, perhaps it is that sorrow and hunger, pity and love, run far deeper in the world than we imagine. They are the underground rivers that the nagas forever traverse; they are the rain that renews us when the right respect has been paid, whether to the nagas or to one another. And if there are no gods, nor any other worlds than this, if there is no such thing as enlightenment or a soul, still there remain those four rivers — sorrow and hunger, pity and love. We humans can survive for terribly long and long without food, without shelter or clothing or medicine, but it is a fact that we will die very soon if the rain does not come.

EARLY STORIES

PITTSBURGH STORIES
(A RECOLLECTION)

"Telephone Call" isn't the first story I ever published, but it is the first I ever got paid for. I wrote it during my freshman year at the University of Pittsburgh, and it's a true story, which is probably why I can live with its being resurrected forty years later. It won *Seventeen Magazine*'s annual fiction contest, and gave me an excuse to quit my summer job. Five hundred dollars went a very long way in 1956.

When I wrote it, I was living in a dormitory called DeSoto Hall, which had once — treasured rumor held — been a hotel of dubious character: in my time it was definitely a rickety, rat-infested firetrap where the University stashed a lot of its freshmen and most of its male black students, whatever year they were in. I remember DeSoto Hall with great tenderness — there really couldn't have been a better place for a cosseted New York Jewish kid, away from home for the first time, to encounter the world. The black kids taught the rest of us to play cutthroat whist; my first-year roommate, a senior, took me down to the Crawford Grill, in the vibrant Hill district, to hear Miles Davis and Cannonball Adderley; and most of the freshmen, black and white, wandered out together in the evenings, to eat dinner at the Greek place on Forbes Street where the waitresses mothered us, to play pinball at the corner cigar store (which still survives), and to try one more hopeless time to buy beer. And the neighborhood was a grimy, gritty blue-collar place where very small criminals took bets and ran numbers, where the Pittsburgh Pirate players could be seen walking to work at the ballpark, and where Pitt's Cathedral of Learning dominated the skyline like an inverted mine shaft. I never dream of the New York City of my childhood, never of the regions of California and the Pacific Northwest I've lived in; but every once in a while I still dream Pittsburgh.

A distraught girl called DeSoto Hall one afternoon in the spring of 1956. I wasn't the one who first picked up the pay telephone in the tiny lounge with its warped Ping-pong table and its sprung green chairs whose splitting vinyl upholstery could actually cut you, but I took my turn when the receiver was wearily handed over to me. The rest followed as the story recounts it, including the cleaning woman's attempt to comfort the girl.

The only other thing perhaps worth mentioning is the most obvious: that "Telephone Call" was written entirely under the influence of *The Catcher in the Rye*. At seventeen I was very consciously trying to put aside the romantic fantasies of my youth, and to write stories about people like the people I was meeting every day in Pittsburgh. And in 1956 it seemed to me, and many other literary adolescents, that the only way to write real people was in the manner of J. D. Salinger. Artists with strongly marked styles are the most seductive to anyone seeking a voice, as I was. But a true style is a life: unique, theft proof. Mannerisms aren't style.

My Salinger crush didn't survive my sophomore year; by the time I wrote "My Daughter's Name Is Sarah," I had already discovered Robert Nathan in the Carnegie Library. Not that you can particularly tell it from this story, as you certainly can from *A Fine and Private Place* a few years later, but the influence is already there in the pacing and the conscious understatement. The story is loosely based on one that my mother told me about her older sister and their father, my gentle teacher/writer grandfather Avrom Soyer. It was the first time I had ever attempted to write from the point of view of a much older person, speaking out of experience as far from my own as it could have been. Three of my mother's brothers became painters, and I grew up in a Bronx apartment hung with their sketches and oil portraits of a white-bearded man with sad, thoughtful eyes. I was trying, however clumsily, to listen to those paintings.

I wrote "Sarah" in 1958, as a member of Edwin L. Peterson, Jr.'s writing class. "Pete" was a small, wiry, red-faced, utterly unpretentious man who loved books and trout-fishing pretty much equally, and who was at once so patient and so stubbornly pushy a teacher that our class won four of the five top places in *The Atlantic Monthly*'s annual college writing contest that year. "Sarah" came in third. The next year, Pete was asked — with, I do hope, some embarrassment — not to enter any of his students in the contest. He was that good, that lovely man.

I'm very glad to include these stories here, juvenilia as they are. The boy who wrote them still lives inside me, and he was always so excited and so proud to see his work in print, even in a college magazine. Me, I don't get that excited, not in that way, and generally I'm just as glad to pretend that I never shared his illusions, his awkwardnesses, his vulnerabilities. But he was there first, and he knows something that I don't anymore.

TELEPHONE CALL

Well, anyway, we were sitting around in the lounge, reading and bull shooting and all. Taylor Hall isn't *big* — I mean, it's not luxurious like these color spreads they have on Ivy League colleges — but it's got a nice lounge with a water cooler and a couple of card tables. Also, it's got a pay phone. I mean, it's a *pay* phone, but you don't really pay. What you do is touch your room key to a couple of terminals in the wall, and you hear two clicks. Then the dial tone goes on, and it's just as if you paid — I mean the operator doesn't know anything about it, and you save a heck of a lot of money over a year, what with girls and all.

So I was just sitting and reading — I do a lot of reading — and Marshall was saying that he for one was getting tired of being called a BBI, which is short for Blankety-Blank Independent, inasmuch as the fraternities only had twenty percent of the kids, even if they did have eighty percent of the money, and Hoffman was agreeing with him, and Walker was arguing, because he was always expecting one of these fraternities to rush him. In the middle of *April*, for Pete's sake!

Bailey — he's the maintenance man, sort of like a janitor, cleans up and all — was reading the *Post-Gazette* and not saying anything, and Moose was coming out of his room every ten minutes and saying will you jerks *please* tune it the heck *down*, did we want him to flunk out, and calling us a bunch of wise guys when we laughed at him. Snickered, you know, like Peter Lorre.

So when the phone rang, at first nobody answered it. I mean they *could* have answered it, it wasn't more than six feet away, but everybody thought somebody else was going to answer it and so nobody did. Well, Bailey finally put down his paper and got up and he got the phone. Marshall said, "If it's a girl, I'm in," and Walker said, "If it's a girl, I'm *out*!" and we laughed. Bailey waved at us and we got quiet and listened.

First, Bailey said, "Hello? Taylor Hall," and then he said, "Who?" Then he said, "You must have the wrong number, ma'am." Then he listened a bit, and then said, "Well, that's this number, but there's nobody here by that name." Then he frowned a little and said, "Wait a minute, ma'am," and he covered the phone with his hand and said, "Anybody named Mike McCullough live here?" as though he really didn't believe it.

Marshall said, "Nope," and Hoffman said, "There's this new guy that moved into room three-oh-seven a week — maybe two weeks ago. Is he McCullough?"

I said, "That's Schmitz," and we all looked at Bailey and sort of shrugged. So he turned back to the phone and said, "No, I'm sorry, ma'am, no Mike McCullough living here." Then he waited and finally said, "Lady, I'm the maintenance man, and I know every guy in here and there's no Mike McCullough."

So he listened a long time, and he tried to interrupt a couple of times. Then he said, "Just a minute," and he covered the phone again and said to us, "Can you beat it! She wants I should read her the ever-loving room list." Hoffman said, "Mightn't be such a bad idea," and Bailey just glared at him and said, "There's no Mike McCullough in this dorm." So I thought, what the heck, and I said, "Let me take it," and Bailey just shrugged and handed me the phone and said, "Hang up on her if she gets fresh." Then he went and sat down again with his paper.

I said, "Hello?" into the phone, and this girl's voice on the other end said, "Hello, Mike?" I said, "No, I'm sorry, but there isn't any Mike McCullough in this dorm. Maybe he lives over in Graduate House or one of the frat houses."

You know, I bet she was a blonde. Anyway, she sounded like one. She had this sort of high voice, nice but kind of high, and to me that means a blonde every time. I don't know, they just always sound like that. So she said, "Oh, that's silly. He told me often enough he lives at Taylor Hall." Then she sort of gasped suddenly, and said, "He hasn't moved out, has he?"

Gee, I'm glad I didn't have to tell her he had, not the way she sounded. What I did tell her was, "Look he hasn't moved out because he never moved in. You sure he said Taylor Hall?"

So she said, real quick, "Oh, yes," and then she didn't say anything for a minute. Then she said, all of a sudden, "Oh, I forgot," and she laughed. "He told me that he told the boys at the dormitory not to say he was in. That is, he said he had to study and he didn't want to be, you know, interrupted." She laughed again, and then she said, "But it's okay. Tell him it's Linda calling."

I ask you. What the heck do you say to something like that? I mean it threw me way off. So I just said the first dopey thing that came to mind. I said, "Linda who?" Dumb, I guess, but I couldn't think of anything else to say. So she said, kind of — well, not mad, but kind of snappish — she said, "Linda Fox, of course he doesn't know any other Linda."

Well, after that, I'd had it. So I put my hand over the phone and said to the guys, "Brother, it's like banging your head against a stone wall. Here, you take it," and I held it out to them. I mean, I didn't hold it out to anyone *definite*, I just figured one guy'd think I meant it for him and he'd take it.

Walker took it. He thought he was pretty darn smooth with the women, and I tell you he really did have a pretty good line. He had this deep, smooth voice and I guess it sounded darn good over a telephone. I guess you got sick of it after a while, but I don't know. I know *I* did.

So Walker picked up the phone and said, "Hello?" You know the way a phone operator says, "Ni-yun, ni-yun, ni-yun"? Well, that's how Walker said "Hello."

Then he said, "I *am* sorry, but there isn't any Mike McCullough here. Won't somebody else do?" I was surprised as the devil when he didn't say, "Like me," but I guess he forgot.

I guess she said no, because he said, not quite so smooth, "Well, I'm awfully sorry, but he doesn't live here." Then he said, "No, I'm sure I know everybody in Taylor Hall, and the only way Mike McCullough could be living here would be in the woodwork."

He must have been surprised when she didn't laugh her fool head off, because he said, "Hey, are you crying? Is that you crying? Well, I *wish*, I really *wish* he lived here, but — " and then he cut off sharp.

He turned around with his face all red, and he put his hand over the phone and said, slow and puzzled, "She called me a stinking liar."

So Marshall got up, and he said, "I think she's one heck of a judge of character. Gimme the phone," and *he* took over. Well, by that time, she must have been *bawling*, because Marshall just kept saying in this worried voice, "Look, don't cry. *Please* don't cry! Look, if you'll just take it easy and stop crying, we'll talk it out." Honest, that was all he said, after "Hello."

Well, after he gave up, just about everybody got into the act. We've got thirty-three guys in Taylor Hall, and I don't say all of them got on the phone, but a couple went twice. Schmitz, the new kid, came in and took a whack at it, and then he came over and sat down next to me. We were in Bio 3 together.

He said, "She just keeps crying and saying she's gotta talk to Mike McCullough. *You* know any McCulloughs?" and I said I didn't. So Schmitz said, "Well the way she's going, if she can't get him, the FBI can't," and then Annie, the cleaning woman, got on the phone.

Well, she said, "Now, you just take it easy, honey, and stop crying." You know, motherly as all get-out. The thing was, she *looked* like somebody's mother; you know, short and fat, and she has gray hair and blue eyes. A woman like that, I mean you'd have been surprised if she wasn't somebody's mother.

So she said, very soothing, "Is Taylor Hall the only address he gave you?" and she waited and said, "Well, you know, this isn't the only Taylor Hall in the world. Maybe he meant the one at Penn State." We all sat up fast, and she waved us back to our chairs and said into the phone, "'Yes, I believe there *is* one at Penn State. Well there's no harm in trying, and if you don't get him there, you can call back here. Maybe he's supposed to move in and we don't know it yet."

Well, then we heard the click all over the room, and Annie just stood there, looking at the phone in her hand. Finally, she hung it up, and Hoffman said, "I got a brother at Penn State, and there's no Taylor Hall there." And Padrias said, "And nobody's gonna move in here with the term darn near over." And everybody nodded, and said *they* had buddies at Penn State, so Annie just raised her hands, kind of tired, and said, "I know. I know, but she's been tying up the phone for nearly an hour and. . ." Then she stopped, and then she said, "and anyway, you can't tell," and she took her mop and went out.

So somebody made a crack about Ed Walker, *alias* Mike McCullough, and that started us off, and we laughed like heck for about five minutes straight. Then it sort of trickled off to nothing, and nobody said anything until Marshall said, "Sounds like a mean son of a gun," and Walker said at the same time, "Pretty smart stunt, though," and they glared at each other, but nothing came of it, and we just didn't talk much for a while.

Well, we waited around for about ten or fifteen minutes, sort of waiting for the phone to ring again, but it didn't, so after a while, all of us got up and went downstairs to play Ping-pong.

My Daughter's Name is Sarah

My name is Elias Reiner and I have a daughter named Sarah and we live in an apartment on Batterman Street. That sounds a little like the jump-rope game the children play in the afternoons. I have seen Sarah do it, jumping up and down while two other girls turn the rope, her eyes closed with concentration, chanting, "My-name-is-Sarah-and-my-father-is-Elias-and-we-live-on-Batterman-Street." She is very fond of jumping rope, and I know that if ever I want to buy her a present and can't think of anything, a jump rope is always good. Other girls just use lengths of clothesline, but Sarah has three jump ropes with handles.

The street is very quiet now in the sun. Schwartz's fruit truck went by ten minutes ago. Schwartz leaned out the window and yelled, "*Hoyaaaaa — peaches! Hoyaaaaa — peaches!*" but no one came out to buy. The old women sit in the sun and talk about their children. A boy goes past on a bicycle and the women's eyes follow him. "Why isn't he in school?" they say, and "Since when do they get out so early, all of a sudden?" and "I know that boy. His mother is a yenta." The boy hunches over the handlebars and disappears around the corner.

It is a lovely day, so beautiful I am a little sad. I get a glass of milk out of the icebox and sit down at the window to watch for Sarah, when she comes home from school. I have just gotten home myself, from Queens college where I teach two courses in Hebrew. It is a good job, and I am happy in it. I still speak with an accent, but the students do not mind. Many of them speak Hebrew very well, and sometimes I conduct the whole class in Hebrew.

It is two-thirty now. At three o'clock the children will come home. They will run up the street, calling to each other, snatching the girls' caps and tossing them back and forth, swinging their books held together by old skate straps. They will come, beautiful and laughing, and as inexorable, in their way, as army ants. And somewhere in the middle of them will be Sarah. When I see her from the window it will be a little hard to breathe for a moment, and I will want to go down and meet her and walk the rest of the way with her.

She wouldn't like that, though. She would not like it if she knew that I sit at the window every day to watch her come home. She would look patient and say, "Papa, *nobody* does that anymore. Not in the sixth grade." And she would be right, of course.

When I see her coming, I will go to the icebox again and get a glass of milk for her, and some cookies. She likes one kind of cookie very much; it is all marshmallow and chocolate. Moise, down on Tremont, always saves a box or two for her. She will come flying down the hall, drop her books on a chair, call "Papa, I'm home," and sit down immediately at the table. I will come out of the living room — I always go there just before she comes, and look busy — and say, "Hello, Sarah."

"Hello, Papa," she will say, with her mouth full of cookies.

"Have a good day?" I will ask casually.

"It was all right." She will look up. "Harry Spector got in trouble again."

This is not news to me. I have never met Harry Spector but, according to Sarah, if he does not get into trouble in class it is because he is not feeling well.

"His mother has to come to class," Sarah will say.

"She must live there."

Sarah will giggle. "I got 87 on the geography test."

"Wonderful. Did you remember about Australia?"

"Uh-huh. Can I have another cookie?"

I will give her one, and she will dip it in the milk. "Marilyn said the funniest thing today," and she will tell me what Marilyn Fine, her best friend, said. Then she will go out to play, and I will watch her in the street until she turns the corner. I will start to make supper.

No, I had forgotten. Today will be different. I slap my forehead. How can one man be so stupid? Today is the last day of school, and Sarah's class is having a party to celebrate and say goodbye. How could I have forgotten, with Sarah talking about nothing else for two weeks? It's a good thing I remembered before she came home.

I bought her a dress for the party. Children can be cruel to a poorly dressed child. Sarah does not know that. She is not cruel herself, and no one has ever been cruel to her. It's a nice dress, dark blue with a sort of white trimming to set off Sarah's black hair. I bought it at Klein's to surprise her. I was afraid she would want to wear it every day and spoil it for the party, but she put it away in the closet until today. "I want Eddie to see me in a brand-new dress," she explained. "I want him to know that I wore it specially for him."

There is a boy named Eddie Liebowitz in Sarah's class, and she loves him. I do not question this for a moment. As much as an eleven-year-old girl can love, my daughter Sarah loves Eddie Liebowitz. I do not think he knows she loves him. I saw them walking home together once. Eddie walked looking straight ahead, talking to Sarah without turning his head. He is a good-looking boy, dark-haired and slim, with an easy way of walking. Sarah walked with her eyes on the ground, kicking a pebble in front of her, occasionally looking at Eddie and looking away again very quickly. On the corner of Batterman some friends called Eddie and he ran off to join them. Sarah stood on the corner and looked after him. The children pressed around her and jostled her and stepped on her feet, but she stood there and would not move until he was out of sight.

She has talked a great deal about Eddie all year. "He's not like any other boy in the class, Papa," she said once. "They're all creeps except Eddie."

"Creep?" I said. "What is a creep?"

I know what *creep* means, and Sarah knows I know. I tease her sometimes, about her friends and their customs and fads and slang. When I see her with them, going to the movies or sitting on a stoop in the spring afternoons I often feel very far away from her. So I make a joke out of it and make her laugh.

That particular time, she talked so much about Eddie that I finally said, "You must like him very much." She looked down at her cereal, said, "Uh-huh" in a small voice, and began to eat very fast. I did not tease her about Eddie anymore, and I never bring him up unless she wants to talk about him.

I look out the window and think about the party in Sarah's class. It must be almost over now. "We all chipped in a quarter," Sarah said this morning, "and Mrs. Glazer bought a lot of jellybeans and Tootsie Rolls and potato chips and stuff. And some Coca-Cola," she added, "because potato chips make you thirsty."

"Will you do anything at this party," I asked, "besides eat?"

Sarah brushed some bread crumbs into her left hand with the

edge of her right hand and swallowed them. "Uh-huh. We're going to dance."

I pretended to be shocked. "So? Since when do you dance in school, where you're supposed to get an education?"

"Oh, *Papa!*" Sarah has a wonderful laugh. It is wholehearted and without fear. "It's not a *real* dance. I mean, it is, but — look, I'll show you." She pushed her chair back and got up. "Come on, I'll show you. Mrs. Glazer taught us."

"In your bathrobe?" I was ironing her party dress.

"Come *on*, Papa." She stamped her foot lightly.

I unplugged the iron. "All right. So show your poor father where his taxes are going. What do I do?"

"The girls stand against the wall," Sarah said, "and Mrs. Glazer puts on a record that goes *dee-dum-dum, dee-dum-dum, dum-dee-dee-dum-dee-dum-dee-dum.* Then the boys pick out partners —" she held out her hands and I took them "— and we dance." We waltzed around in a circle at arm's-length. Sarah's eyes were half-shut, and she was *dum-dee-dumming* happily until I stepped on her foot. She yelped and broke away.

I dropped to one knee. "Are you all right? Let me see."

"I'm all right. You have big feet."

We laughed together, and I got up. "Well, you won't be dancing with me. Whom will you dance with, Sarala?"

"Eddie," said Sarah, softly but clearly. "I'm going to dance with Eddie."

"What Eddie," I teased her. "Eddie who?"

"*Papa!* Eddie Liebowitz!"

"Oh, *that* Eddie. Will he pick you out?"

"Of course he will." Oh, she was so calm and sure.

I began to iron her dress again. "Finish your breakfast. You'll be late." Sarah looked at the clock and began to gulp her milk. "Slow, slow! You will burp right in the middle of the dance and wouldn't that be lovely?"

Sarah began to laugh and choked over her milk. I handed her a napkin and she wiped her face and got up. I finished ironing and gave her the dress. She went into her bedroom, and I heard her singing as she dressed. I put the dishes in the sink and cleaned off the table.

I went into the hall and called into Sarah's bedroom. "You know, Sarala, this dance your Mrs. Glazer taught you would be very popular in Samoa."

"Where?" Sarah's voice was muffled.

"Samoa. It is like a tribal dance the boys and girls do there. There is a picture of it in the College — I'll bring it home."

Sarah appeared in the bedroom doorway suddenly. She was wearing the new dress and her best shoes. She had brushed her hair without my reminding her, and she was wearing a necklace of little white beads that I bought her one afternoon, coming home from the College.

"Do I look nice?" she asked.

"Mmmmmm." I squinted my eyes and tilted my head to the side. "Passable, passable." And then I held her close and told her how beautiful she was until she twisted away and said, "Papa, you'll wrinkle my dress."

"God forbid," I said. I took her by the shoulders and looked down at her. "Sarah, Sarala — if anything goes wrong — don't be disappointed." It sounded foolish immediately.

"What do you mean, Papa?"

"Well, I mean — if Eddie does not dance with you —" Sarah began to laugh.

"Papa, who else would he dance with?"

You can never protect the unhurt. You cannot tell them that everyone must be a little afraid to be safe.

"No one, Sarah. I was being silly." I turned back to the kitchen. "Go to school now."

She pattered after me and caught my arm. "There is a girl in the class who'd like Eddie to dance with her. Her name is Tilly Hofberg, and she's a *nebbish*."

Nebbish is a favorite word of ours. We use it to describe a mousy, colorless sort of person. We even have degrees of *nebbishes*. "What kind of a *nebbish* is Tilly Hofberg?"

"A first-class, A-number-one, triple-distilled *nebbish*."

"Triple-distilled?"

"Triple-distilled. She looks at Eddie all day and tries to get close to him in fire drill. Once she even followed him home." She laughed with a sort of cheerful contempt.

"Does he like her?"

"He used to, but he doesn't anymore. Eleanor Frankel told Marilyn and Marilyn told me. Do you think Eddie'll like the necklace?"

"He will love it," I said. "Go now, or you will be late." Sarah kissed me and ran down the hall.

"Your books," I called after her. "You left your books."

"I don't need them," she called over her shoulder as she ran out the door. "I don't need them."

I went to the window and saw her as she crossed the street with Marilyn Fine. They had their arms around each other and they were talking. Sarah's blue dress shone in the sun.

It is almost three o'clock now. In a few minutes the children will be coming home. The old women talk to each other and move their wooden folding chairs to keep in the shade. Engel the junkman goes by, his cart pulled by his old white horse. The children love that horse and call him "Silver." I rest my elbow on the window sill and wait.

Suddenly the street is full of children. They run up the long street singing and shouting, because this is the last day of school. There are so many children. I know some of them by sight now, particularly one fat boy who keeps bumping into the other children. I do not think he means to, but he is clumsy and cannot help himself. I asked Sarah about him once, and she said that he was a fifth-grader and once cried at recess when the children teased him.

I see Sarah. She is walking with Marilyn still. They are talking and I see Sarah laugh. My stomach seems to relax — I did not realize that I had been so worried about her. The party has gone well, and now it is over, and Sarah is coming home. I turn away from the window to get Sarah's milk and cookies. I set them on the table.

I will not ask her about the party. This is something private, and if she wants to tell me, she may. This belongs to her. I go into the living room and take a book from the shelf.

I do not open it, although it is poetry. The door opens. I hear Sarah's footsteps in the hall.

She turns into the kitchen and then turns to the living room. She stands in the doorway, smiling. "Hello, Papa."

"Hello, Sarah."

Silence. She is still smiling. "Papa?

I look at my beautiful daughter. "So?"

Suddenly the smile is gone, and it is like watching the winter come. Sarah's face is pale, and her mouth is trembling. "Papa," she says, and her voice breaks. "Oh, Papa — he went to Tilly!"

Then she is in my arms and crying as I have never heard her cry.

Her whole body is shaking as if a wind had passed over her and her face and hands are so cold. Over and over, "Tilly — he went to Tilly!"

What do you do, what do you do? What am I to tell her, after all? I hold her very tight and say, "Sarah, Sarah, Sarala — this is not the end. Sarah, darling, this is not the end." And I know that it is not the end, because I am grown, and therefore wise. But my daughter Sarah cries as though it were.

Essays

LEARNING A TRADE

During the 1960s, I earned my living primarily by writing for general-interest magazines, especially *Holiday* and the *Saturday Evening Post*, which were part of the long-gone Curtis empire. *Holiday* serialized *I See By My Outfit*, my book about a cross-country journey on a motorscooter, in two issues, paying $8000, which fed and housed me, my first wife, and three small children for close to two years in the hills north of Santa Cruz. As I've said, money really used to go a lot further than it does now.

While I was trying to learn how you make a living and feed people out of nothing but a gift for telling stories, a *Holiday* editor named Harry Sions took a liking to me, and went out of his way to find assignments for me, at times actually letting me suggest them myself. Remembered only as a travel magazine, *Holiday* in the days of editors like Sions, Ted Patrick and John D. Weaver was in fact a wondrous sanctuary for nearly any type of classy nonfiction. Among other pieces, I wrote a long essay on the Bronx, where I had grown up, a review of John Barth's novel *Giles Goat-boy*, one of the earlier studies of J.R.R. Tolkien (which later became the foreword to *The Tolkien Reader*), and the two reprinted here. The third is something else altogether.

I enjoyed freelance work, and I got reasonably good at the trade; but even at my best, I was never in a class with the real ones, the people like Joseph Mitchell, Joan Didion, Ken Lamott, Edward Hoagland, Arnold Hano, or the aforementioned John Weaver. There was no comparison in range or quality between their professional bodies of work and my occasional bread-and-butter gigs though I'm sure I thought so at the time. But I was at least discovering what real professionalism meant, and what story means, and precisely what a maximum length of 3000 words means. Harry and John couldn't make a great journalist out of me, but they taught me how to put bread on the table, and for that I will always be grateful.

"My Last Heroes" was, obviously, a young man's labor of love. Nothing much needs to be said about it, except that Warren Spahn pitched one last year for the San Francisco Giants, and in the course of time was deservedly named to the Baseball Hall of Fame. He's still alive at this writing; but Georges Brassens died of cancer in 1981 at the age of sixty. Not long after "My Last Heroes" was published, he recorded a song about World War I called "Les Deux Oncles," in which he remarked, "Uncle Martin liked the Tommies, Uncle Gaston liked the Teutons — each one died for his friends. I, who like no one, I'm still here." The song, which went on to discuss the bitter waste and utter meaninglessness of the deaths of Uncle Martin and Uncle Gaston, created an immense scandal in France, and there was no more talk of nominating Brassens to the Académie Française. In the tiny Santa Cruz restaurant where I sang his songs every weekend for twelve years, I always sang "Les Deux Oncles."

As for "D. H. Lawrence In Taos," I still remember enjoying the people I met in the course of researching the article a good deal more than I've ever enjoyed Lawrence's passionate posturing. Writing this, more than thirty years later, I realize that I remember Lou and Bea Ribak, Dorothy Brett, Joseph O'Kane Foster, Bill and Rachel Hawk, John Evans and Claire Spencer far better than I do most of the Lawrence books I've read; which, for good or ill, tells you something about me, if not about D. H. Lawrence. For that matter, Taos itself turned out to have far more importance in my life than Lawrence, or even good old *Holiday* — but that's another story. Anyway, I'm glad to see this one here.

"The Poor People's Campaign," is the best magazine writing I ever did. Until now, it's never been published anywhere. The *Saturday Evening Post* commissioned the piece in 1968, after Martin Luther King, Jr. was killed, but they folded before they could run it. I didn't even have a copy; it was John Weaver who found it in his own archives and sent it to me. John and I actually ran into each other at Resurrection City — he had covered the equally heartbreaking, equally doomed Bonus Marchers' Campaign of 1932, as a young reporter, and was returning on his own out of a fierce desire to see whether anything very much had changed in governmental and cultural attitudes toward the powerless of this country. He didn't think so.

And I don't think anything has changed myself, not in any way that matters. For all the dated references in the story, for all the undeniably improved social conditions for black people in the South today, it seems to me that today's America not only gives far less of a rat's ass about the poor than it did thirty years ago, but can no longer be bothered even to pretend that it cares. Lyndon Johnson, sins and corruption and Vietnam and all, really did care, and believed more genuinely in his war on poverty than he ever did in that other one that had crippled his administration by that summer of 1968. The Poor People's Campaign wouldn't get anywhere near the Mall or the Reflecting Pool today, or the Lincoln Memorial either.

MY LAST HEROES

When I was very young, every grownup was a hero. It's been all downhill since then, and I have only two left. One of them is Warren Spahn. I have loved Spahn since I was ten and he was twenty-eight, pitching against the Giants on a spring afternoon. I think he lost, but it didn't matter. Victory was in him; it was not something that happened to him. His true opponent was something greater than the New York Giants, and it was my adversary as well. Even then I knew that I was going to be a writer and not a pitcher, but when you're ten it's the same thing.

That was sixteen years ago — a pitcher's lifetime, and a child's. Spahn has lost his hair and his fastball in that time, and I have certainly lost something. Both of us have gained in craft and cunning, but it's hardly the same as being ten and twenty-eight in the spring with your limitations yet to be learned. Every April I prayed for Spahn to win twenty games one more time. "Next year I'll be old enough so things like that won't matter anymore." He kept on winning, at thirty and thirty-five and forty. I used to see him a lot when I was going to college in Pittsburgh, because he always worked against the Pirates, and you could get into the bleachers for nothing after the sixth inning. I dragged a lot of girls out of the movies into the strange green daylight of night games to stand on tiptoe and see my love: long neck tough and wrinkled, body maybe thickening just a little, the man himself looking like an amiable tenpin in locker-room photographs, but still *cutting* through the haze and the hollering when he moved to throw a white ball.

Neither the New York Giants nor the Boston Braves exist anymore, and big-league baseball is in violation of the whole Bill of Rights, the Sherman Act and the Geneva Convention. Spahn had a terrible season with Milwaukee last year. They ceased to believe in him and kept taking him out around the fifth inning; and after the season ended they sold him to the New York Mets, than which no greater expression of corporate disbelief exists. Yet this year I made my April wish for him again, because when he goes, the only link remaining between me and the ten-year-old boy in the Polo Grounds, which is gone too, will be whatever of that boy survives in me now. To have a hero is to give yourself away, yourself at a certain moment of need. It's as dangerous as voodoo.

If Spahn is, in a sense, the custodian of my childhood, the keeper of my graceless youth is Georges Brassens. Brassens is a big, moustached Frenchman from the Midi who writes songs and sings them. Nobody writes songs like his, even in a country where they have a tradition of sung poetry going back to the 12th century. Brassens's songs are about gorillas who rape judges, uncles who marry Death, shepherdesses who suckle kittens, old peasants who die of natural causes, and the navels of policemen's wives. They are poems about umbrellas and ducks and gravediggers and the wind. Once you hear them, they seem to have always been there.

The part of myself that belongs to Georges Brassens is the me of the Pittsburgh winter when I lost my girl. I remember the evening very well, for I spent two hours talking to her on the telephone, explaining that experience had matured me since that last awful Saturday night, but that she'd better grab me now before I matured right out of her universe. But she had a new man. I think that I quoted Catullus as I hung up: *"Insane one, do you know what you have thrown away?"* Bang. And that goes for your whole damn family, Miss Pulcher. It was all very silly, but my stomach ached. I wanted to get drunk, but that seemed like overacting, so I went to the Carnegie Library instead. I majored in the Carnegie Library. They had a room on the second floor where you could listen to records, and they stayed open until nine most nights. I took all my stomachaches to the library.

I wonder now why I decided to listen to a record of Patachou singing French songs. I didn't know any French, and emotionally I was on a Spanish kick which took such forms as translating "Mack the Knife" into Spanish. Patachou herself was a discovery. She had a good tart voice, a woman's voice, and she sang French with casual purity. But eight of the songs she sang were by Brassens; and I have never heard her sound quite that good again. As good, perhaps, but never in the same way.

They were his earliest songs — "La Chasse Aux Papillons, J'ai Rendezvous Avec Vous, La Prière" — and in some ways they are still his best. They have the strength that sometimes comes from simplicity, and a lightness that I think belongs to the time when no one had ever heard of Georges Brassens. I had never heard anything like them before; and yet, as I listened, I felt myself smiling with recognition. They were the songs I had been writing in my head all my life, as I know that I wrote certain books and poems when I read them; as I invented cats and giraffes, and Spahn taut to throw. I probably didn't say, "Oh yes, that's it," not aloud, but I smiled, and I forgot about the girl, yesterday's that's-it. Not for forever, but for that evening.

Brassens sang with Patachou on one track, a song called "Maman, Papa." He has a strange voice, always a little unexpected: deep and hoarse, a funny voice. This must surely be the only recording he ever made with an orchestra, and he sang as though he were trying not to hear it; doggedly behind the beat, and so close to going flat that I felt myself leaning toward him to keep him on key, a kind of soul-English. He growled over the lowest notes, devouring them, and his drawling accent clashed as much with Patachou's painfully beautiful Parisian French as the quality — the idea — of his voice did with the sound of flutes and clarinets. A funny voice; and absolutely real, perfectly present. There was nothing between me and it. Brassens sang:

> Papa, papa, il n'y eut pas entre nous,
> Papa, papa, de tendresse ou de mots doux.
> Pourtant on s'aimait bien qu'on ne se l'avoua pas,
> Papa, papa, papa, papa.

"Papa, there was never any tenderness between us, nor any kind words; yet we did love one another, though we never said so." The voice and the music were alike: gentle and ferocious and ridiculous all at once, making the sorrowful words sound funny. All of Brassens's songs are like that, like the music of the Shee in Yeats's "The Stolen Bride" — "And never was piping so sad, and never was piping so gay."

I began looking for him then, without ever knowing what I wanted to ask him. I found a record of his in New York, on which, for the first time, I heard him accompany himself on the guitar. He played without show, carelessly, but with the authority beyond error that only real musicians have; the mixture of skill and delight that can make the simplest chord change exciting. The guitar was another contradiction woven into his music — it lightened his harshest songs and drove the gentle dance tunes along at a fierce, ominous pace. "Les Amoureux des Bancs Publics" is a kindly song about budding lovers who ignore the sidelong glances of the righteous passers-by; but with that guitar behind it, the innocuous java rhythm closed in tighter and tighter around the young lovers, and by the end of the song "they had lived the best part of their love on one of those famous benches," and now they were the righteous passers-by. Listening to Brassens's guitar I knew that I wanted to play like that, and sing like that, and write songs like that. I thought then that they were separate skills, to be mastered separately.

Once, that same winter, a friend of mine got me a blind date with a French girl so that her roommate could go out with him in good conscience. The girl was very nice and so was I, which doomed the evening, and we both knew it as soon as we met. The four of us had dinner together, went to a movie, and then came back to the girls' apartment, where my friend and his girl disappeared into another room. They had a curious air of duelists, I remember. The French girl and I sat on a sofa so high that our feet didn't touch the floor. "Let's talk about pragmatism," she said, being a philosophy student. She was such a nice girl. I asked her if she knew any Brassens songs, and with great relief she sang me all the ones I knew and some I'd never heard. When there were noises in the other room, she sang louder. She sang until my friend came out, ready to go home. I never saw her again, but I think of her sometimes, sitting up straight with her legs hanging down, singing Brassens's love songs for me.

Then suddenly I graduated from college, and I went to Europe for a year or so. Paris, mostly. It was a stupid time; it has that kind of flavor, anyway, when I think about it — the taste that makes you wriggle and spit. *Ah no, my God, was that me, that cold puppet? Oy, schnook.* It was a lonesome, stupid time, and if I learned anything from it, it doesn't show. I would manage things better now, but not much better.

I knew no French, and I had no friends. I could feel myself disappearing day by day, until it seemed to me that I was no more than a pair of eyes floating through the streets of Paris, speechless, shadowless, seeing some things but making no sense of them. But in the evenings I went to see Brassens at the Olympia or the Bobino, and when he came walking onstage, head down, clutching his guitar by the neck, his moustache like great wings, then somehow I had a voice again, and being. I even glanced around in my seat and smiled at the people sitting near me, certain that I could talk to them.

He would take a drink from the carafe on the piano, put his left foot up on an old chair, and sing those songs in that voice, in this world. Graying, wild-haired, sweating in the lights, he had no stage presence; he was just *there*, like an animal, like the bear he is always compared to, like the sound of his voice and his guitar. Between songs he wandered in the space between the chair, the piano and his bass-fiddle accompanist, who always whispered the few words that seemed to turn him slowly back to the lights and the applause. When he was finished he walked off with the steps of a man trying not to run. He never gave encores, and he never bowed.

"I'm a weed, good people," Brassens sang. "You can't eat me, and you can't stick me in a bouquet. I'm a weed, good people. I grow wild in your neglected gardens." I live in a world where entertainment is a way of life, where art and politics are both part of show biz, and in this world most performers are not human beings at all but images created by committees. So I believe in committees, but not in performers, and I guard my credulity as closely as I can, because that's what all the committees are after. But Brassens smiled into his guitar and sang, "*La, la, la, la, la, la, la, la,*" and (like Spahn, making something solitary out of that silly, corrupt game) he cut through the loud shadows that all beg, "Love me, love me, keep me alive." He was frightened, and he was fighting to stay human with every move he made, but he was not afraid of being unloved or alone. "*C'est immoral, et c'est, comm' ça,*" he sang, and the sound he made was both sad and gay.

When I came back home, folk music was just becoming popular, and almost everyone I knew played the guitar, at varying degrees of speed. There was a party every night, somewhere, and at the center of it someone invariably sang "Railroad Bill," "Freight Train" or "San Francisco Bay Blues." It was an interesting time, especially if you liked "Freight Train," but I discovered at the parties that my repertoire consisted of sixty-two Brassens songs and nothing else. I liked the others, but I couldn't sing them; they might as well have been in a foreign language. I had learned French to understand those Brassens songs, when I couldn't learn it to talk to other people, and I had sung them over and over until they began to blossom in my mind, a word at a time. For whatever it was worth, I had earned them, and they were my folklore. When something truly belongs to you, you become briefly aware how little else does, how much is bought or borrowed or handed down or, most likely, just accumulated, like dust and toys. You can only keep — or give away — what belongs to you.

Later someone who'd been to those parties told me, "You put us all down, you know, with that French stuff."

"You're crazy," I said. "I was out of it. I was an embarrassment. I used to go home wishing to God I'd never learned to play the guitar."

"No, you had a good bag going," he said. "You'd sit there and you'd say, 'This is a song by Georges Brassens. It's about a duck.' It was pretty hard to follow with 'Wildwood Flower.'"

Brassens was my bag, my bit, my thing, my hangup; as he still is, really. The sound of him on a record can still make me stop whatever I'm doing and say softly, "Ah, that wicked old sonofabitch. That nut." It can also make me feel like crying. I'll sing his complete works for anything that moves, translating each song carefully to explain the dislocated clichés, the quotations from Villon and the Pléiade and the other strange things that Brassens does with words. Sitting alone with my guitar, my fingers melt through the chord patterns that have never come to bore me, and I pick out his tunes to hear — almost to see — them cut their lean shapes into the air. And when I sing them, alone or for others, the special joy that is the other side of crying goes roaring around inside me, making me smile foolishly.

Recently he's been nominated for membership in the Académie Française, which would make him an immortal by definition. It's a great honor, but in a curious way it's also a little like being sold to the New York Mets. Live burial. I wonder if he'll accept it (he wrote a cockeyed song-play years ago which contains a charming and profound obscenity about the Académie), but I don't worry about the possibility of his contamination by canonization, as I would have once. His sound has remained the same over the years; a little darker, perhaps, but as unauthorized and unfashionable as ever. One of his latest songs addresses itself both to the young who look upon their elders as *cons* (let's say jerks), and to the old who hold the same opinion of their children, warning them all, as "one balanced between two ages,"

> *Le temps ne fait rien à l'affaire,*
> *Quand on est con, on est con.*

"Time has nothing to do with it. Once a jerk, always a jerk." The song skewered one of my dearest illusions when I first heard it — the one about how I'll understand when I'm a grownup — but it's become curiously comforting when I look in the mirror. Only a man who knew himself for a *con* could have written it.

And yet it took me a long time to learn the one thing Brassens had to teach me. As I have said, I wanted to sing and write and play and even look like that, and when it came home to me that it was all one thing, all part of the same man, then I wanted to be Brassens. He made such a perfect me. I have read that Brassens used to feel the same way about François Villon. Perhaps it was Villon who reconciled Brassens to being Brassens, in the same way that listening to Brassens these days often makes me happier about being myself and making my own sound. *Moi, qui ne suis pas capitaine,* as he sings so proudly. I, who am no captain, no hero.

Still, it is always the idea you love, no matter how much it seems to be the fact, the person. There is a Rene Clair movie, *Porte des Lilas,* in which Brassens plays a character referred to only as L'Artiste: a silent man, watching and thinking, playing the guitar in cafes and at dances for pocket money, and spending most of his time in his little house with his cats, his books, his wine and an occasional worthless friend. The opening shot of the picture is still vivid in my mind: the rainy autumn streets of a workingman's *quartier,* and Brassens's voice far away, singing. The next shot shows him sitting on a table in a tiny bistro, crouched in an old overcoat and a muffler, "playing music to empty pockets," like blind Raftery. He looks old and wild and strayed from somewhere, sometime. Hesitantly and wearily, he is singing his most beautiful song, "Au Bois de Mon Coeur."

"In the woods of Meudon, Clamart, Vincennes, St. Cloud, there are little flowers, and in the woods of my heart I have my friends. They know that I'm a better man than I'm named; they're not afraid to drink my water when all my wine is gone. Each time I get married they come to the wedding with me, and each time I die they follow my funeral." That's my song still; and when I close my eyes, that's still me sitting on the table singing it, though I know better. I can't pitch, either.

D. H. Lawrence in Taos

He wasn't here very long. He came to Taos for the first time in September of 1922, left for Mexico the following March, and didn't return for a year. Then, in October, 1924, he went to Mexico again. He came back the next spring, his body devastated by tuberculosis and malaria, and he stayed until September. Then he went back to England because his American visa had expired, and he died in Vence, France, on March 2, 1930. His ashes were brought back to the Taos ranch five years later, and buried there.

In the legend of D. H. Lawrence, the names of cities and countries, continents and hemispheres, resound like stations of the cross. Nottingham, Icking, Lago di Garda, Ebenhausen, Gollo della Spezia, Sussex, Oaxaca, Villa Mirenda, and so to his death in France. But Taos is the place to which he returned when he knew beyond denial that he was going to die soon; and since we who retell the legend know it all along — as we know what is going to happen to Hector, or Oedipus, or John Henry — the name is informed by the light of doom.

What did happen to him here? He seems, in this pause in his voyage, to have been living out an old and cherished fantasy of neverland where he and a few close friends would live together, working and loving, involved with their work and each other and the earth, and nothing more. The idea had a name — Rananim — and he never came any closer to achieving it than he did on the ranch in Taos.

Lawrence in Taos. *Lorenzo in Taos*. It is a book title, and it sounds as though it should be the name of an opera or a ballet. A ballet would be better. The program notes could explain it: This is the legend of a great artist and three women. They all outlived him.

Frieda Lawrence, Mabel Dodge Luhan, Dorothy Brett. The wife;

the wealthy woman who invited him to her Taos to discover her Indians
and herself, and the deaf painter who adored him unquestioningly.
There is a painting by Dorothy Brett that shows the three of them sitting
around a table. Frieda is in the middle, laughing, a cigarette stuck to
her lower lip. Mabel Luhan is in the left foreground: dark hair cut like
a cap; clever, watchful eyes. Brett sits on the right. She has portrayed
herself as less attractive than the other two, but softer. Lawrence himself
is in the background, writing, looking cramped. The painting is called
Lawrence's Three Fates.

Taos is still a very small town, though it has probably doubled in
size in the last ten or fifteen years. There is only one real intersection,
and the roads are too narrow for the big new cars. The pueblo is only
a little way from the town, and there are always old Indians, wrapped
in blankets, standing on the edges of the central plaza, watching things
happen, watching nothing happen. But the young Indian girls wear
white lipstick and miniskirts.

At La Fonda de Taos, where I stayed, some of Lawrence's paintings
are on display, eight or ten of them. There is a little sign on the front
door, restricting visitors to Adults Only and reminding them that
the paintings were banned in London in 1929. You pay a dollar to be
ushered into a tiny room — somebody's private office — where the
canvases fall on you, seeming bigger and probably worse than they
really are. They are not obscene, not in the least erotic, and they are not
very good either. Only one of them holds me for a little: a leaden-fleshed
Rape of the Sabines, into which Lawrence has painted his own face. It
scowls in a lower corner, looking lonely and envious — not of the act
but of its simplicity — and disgusted with himself for having stopped to
think. The painting, like most of the others, has a $15,000 price tag. It is
beginning to come off the canvas.

When my wife and I were here, we went first to visit Louis and
Beatrice Ribak. They are both painters, dissimilar in their work as
they are in many other ways, but alike in their kindness and in their
dedication. Louis and Bea have lived in Taos since 1944. They never
knew Lawrence, and were only casually acquainted with Frieda during
her last years; but one of their close friends, the novelist Joseph O'Kane
Foster, came over that night, able and delighted to talk about Lawrence.
A young poet named Robert Sward and his wife Diane also came by.
Bob Sward held a D. H. Lawrence Fellowship from the University of

New Mexico last summer, and lived up at the ranch.

"Lawrence was a prophet," said Foster, a thin, birdlike man of about seventy. "He changed my life. I was just out of college with a degree in philosophy when I met him. He made me see that it was all garbage, what I had in my head — that I didn't know a goddamn thing about anything. I started all over after I met Lawrence.

"As a thinker, as a philosopher, he was years ahead of his time. I honestly think that we're just beginning to catch up with Lawrence now, thirty-six years after his death. Today you can't possibly imagine the literary situation when Lawrence began to write. You never even used the *word* 'passion' then, let alone trying to describe it. The whole world of male and female relationships was taboo in art — it's as simple as that. Well, Lawrence changed all that, singlehanded; he broke through and he changed things, and didn't they hate him for it! That's something else you can't imagine — the incredible hatred, the vilification, the persecution. He came to Taos because of the hatred.

"Sex wasn't all of it, though. They called him a sex writer, and of course he took up the challenge, but the real thing was class. Lawrence was forever attacking the English class system, mocking it, chipping away at it. Clifford Chatterly is England in a wheelchair."

He talked all evening, apologizing now and then for his verboseness. There was no need, for he talked well, and it made him seem young.

"Just being around the man was exciting. He loved to argue, and he was really only interested in people who would disagree with him. He was always ill, terribly ill — he weighed eighty-nine pounds when I knew him — but he had tremendous power, tremendous animal magnetism. Yet I don't think he was really sexually attractive to women. Frieda, of course — well, they were in love. They fought continually, physically and in every other way, but they were deeply in love."

The next day we went up to the Lawrence ranch with Bob Sward and the Ribaks. It was a day like a knife: bright and polished and cold. The ranch is about twenty-one miles from Taos, 8,000 feet up on a mountain slope called the Lobo, which is part of the Sangre de Cristo range. The view stretches out like a copper sea in the afternoon light, with the gray-blue sagebrush making shadowy troughs between the hard, slow waves. The sky springs up over it like a live thing, supple and beautiful and indifferent. *St. Mawr* described it all:

> . . . she could watch the vast, eagle-like wheeling of the daylight, that turned as the eagles which lived in the near rocks turned overhead in the blue. . . And sometimes the vast strand of the desert would float with curious undulations and exhalations amid the blue fragility of mountains, whose upper edges were harder than the floating bases.

Bob named the buildings for us. There is the house where Lawrence and Frieda lived: there is Lawrence's pine, Lawrence's garden, Lawrence's Indian oven, where he baked bread. Mabel and Tony Luban lived in the other cottage. This was Dorothy Brett's hut; an unbelievably tiny cell that needed only a few spikes on the door to be an Iron Maiden. They say she made it very charming, though. Tony Luhan painted that buffalo on the ranch house.

They are very well kept up, the little log and adobe houses. The University keeps a permanent crew of caretakers on the land, and at first sight the ranch looks as though Lawrence still lived there. That day, there was even smoke coming from the chimney of his house. The University allows occasional special guests to stay there as well as the fellowship holders.

A man came out as we hesitated near the steps. "Can I help you?" He seemed in his seventies, red-checked and blue-eyed, looking remarkably like Robert Frost. "My name is Garnett," he said. He wore a checked shirt and blue jeans, and his voice was slow and English.

It was David Garnett. There can't be more than one Garnett family in England; the name must be copyrighted. I have a book of stories by his grandfather, Richard Garnett, and I was introduced to Dostoevski by his mother's translations; and his most famous novel, *Lady into Fox*, is one of my favorites. It was like meeting, not a Cro-Magnon man, perhaps, but anyway a passenger pigeon. This man has known everybody — he knew Thomas Hardy. Hardy died only two years before Lawrence, but somehow the difference is a matter of a whole century. A man who knew Thomas Hardy might have known Dickens or Browning. He invited us in.

Inside, it seems a very small place. Bob Sward, who has two children, says that he and his family were quite comfortable; but it's like looking at suits of armor in a museum and trying to fit your giants into them. White walls, beamed roof, a fireplace, a kitchen; a lean, rough-walled bedroom. The roof dominates everything. On a bad day it must have lowered and lowered until people had to go around stooping. There is a sense of visiting a celebrated battleground.

A television set has been installed in the front room! It stands in a corner, looking sullen, as though it were aware of its own grotesqueness and absurdity. I've never seen a TV set look like that before.

David Garnett sat down at a table covered with letters and manuscripts. He is a calm, easy man, comfortable in Lawrence's house at the age of seventy-five.

"I met Lawrence in 1912, when I was twenty years old. He was very gay, with a great gift of mimicry, which — in those days — he used as much against himself as against others. He was forever getting up games of charades, and he used to do turns in which he burlesqued himself as a shy, awkward young man trying to charm his landlady. I liked him very much then.

"This was just after he had run off with Frieda, and they were living in Icking, by the Isar. Frieda couldn't have been more different from Lawrence. She was several years older than he, for one thing, and she was a slow person, without being stupid. She'd puzzle about a thing or a situation and get it wrong, and then she'd puzzle about it some more and get it right. She had been married to an Englishman named Weekley, and they were living in the country, and English provincial life was just not for Frieda. Lawrence had been a pupil of her husband's at the University of Nottingham, and one day he came to lunch with them. He and Frieda looked at each other, and that was that."

He spoke slowly, with amusement but without malice. "I liked him very much, but I broke with him in 1915 because he was trying to run my life. Lawrence had no use for people who weren't followers, but I had my own way to go. There were four girls whom I was quite fond of; old, old friends — I'd known them since I was three or four. Lawrence said they were no good for me, told me to give them up. Well, I gave him up instead.

"Frankly, I think Lawrence ruined himself by taking himself seriously as a thinker. His great gift, it seems to me, was for making you see; for making an atmosphere, a light, an object, so visible that you can never again see it as you were used to. But politically, philosophically, he talked a lot of bosh, really. There was nothing there."

As we were leaving, Louis Ribak asked about the TV set. David Garnett laughed. "It is odd, isn't it? I keep thinking what Lawrence would have made of it. I disconnected the thing long ago."

Afterward we walked up to the little chapel where Lawrence and Frieda are buried. It is on a long hill above the ranch: a cream-colored building with a tall, thin cross standing near the door.

Frieda's headstone is outside; it has an oval photograph of her set into it like a cameo. Inside, there is a low stone railing with two carved doors, and beyond it a kind of altar. Light enters in the front and rear walls. A strange, ugly picture hangs on the right — it is painted on glass and looks like a pulpy, pulsing red flower. On the other wall, over the guest register, are the original French and English papers certifying that the remains of David Herbert Lawrence have been removed from the cemetery at Vence for reburial in the United States.

I call Dorothy Brett, the last survivor of Lawrence's Three Fates. She came to Taos with Lawrence and Frieda when they returned in 1924 — the only one who came, of all the friends he invited to his Rananim — and she has stayed on. "Oh, dear," she says on the phone, with mixed nervousness and impatience. "Oh, dear. Very well, then. You come around in half an hour or so."

She lives in El Prado, a few miles north of Taos; you pass her house on the way to the ranch. It's impossible to miss the house, because there is a big signboard off to one side, with her coat of arms on it. Dorothy Brett (she is always referred to as "the Brett") is a titled lady, the daughter of Viscount Esher, and she has a coat of arms. A dragon and a hippogriff rampant on either side of a shield.

A sign on the door says that she cannot hear the bell, so I swing over a low gate and push the door open. "Yes, you come right in," she says, turning to meet me. Dorothy Brett is stout and white-haired, wearing a painter's smock over a pretty dress. I have seen paintings forty years old that show her as a small-featured, slack-jawed woman with a curious air — perhaps because of her deafness — of disconnection, irrelevance; the way a baby's eyes look before they begin to focus on the world. But now, in her eighties, with her face as lined as a walnut, her eyes have come aware, and her head has weathered into dignity and strength. Dorothy Brett was probably always meant to be old.

Her studio is very bright with flowers and paintings, hats and clothes; pots, purses, lamps, rugs, blankets, Mexican crucifixes, Indian statues. The room might belong to a younger woman. There are one or two drawings of Lawrence; more of Stokowski. A large, hysterical dachshund wants to go out.

"Have you read much about Lawrence?" Dorothy Brett asks. "No? Well, you're well off, then. There have been an immense number of stupid books written about him. One reads them, and when you remember the person and the time, you become so furious and frustrated and sad. So stupid.

"What was he like? He had beautiful manners. He was a very considerate and polite man with beautiful instinctive manners. People liked him immediately: bus conductors, children, peasant women in Oaxaca. It was a delight to go riding or walking with him — he saw everything, he made everything so interesting. He had his rages, certainly — all red-haired people do — but then, who doesn't? And you'd be flying into rages, too, if you lived with Frieda. She was this great, gusty, earthy, mothering sort, utterly unlike Lawrence. She had nothing of his observation, none of his insights — she was really a peasant herself, for all her aristocratic ancestry. And yet she had something, that something he just couldn't do without."

In the matter of the Lawrence's celebrated battles, Dorothy Brett is vigorously on Lawrence's side, as she always was. "Of course he fought with her. Frieda was a great bully, and she wanted to be the center of attraction, the first fiddle, as she had been all her life before she met Lawrence. And around him, she was definitely the second fiddle. He was the main attraction, he was the one people came to see. She hated that, and she tried to keep him all to herself, isolated with her. And he got bored, very bored."

She relents a little, and smiles with a touch of grimness. "Of course, we all three wanted him all for ourselves. We wanted to have secrets with him, do you see? But once he was dead — once the bone of contention was removed — we women became much better friends than we had been." David Garnett suggested at the ranch that Lawrence's famous rages may well have prolonged his life by shooting massive doses of adrenaline through his doomed body. Dorothy Brett nods. "I wouldn't be at all surprised. Although I think Lawrence would be alive today if he'd stayed in Taos. I remember the first time he came back here from old Mexico — he was simply pea-green. He was dreadfully ill. And within a month he was writing and working. I do wish he'd stayed here.

"I kept the ranch up for years, hoping he'd come back. But when he wanted to come back, Frieda didn't; and when she wanted to, then he didn't and finally it was too late."

Dorothy Brett rises and turns toward the window. The dachshund is all over her, thinking that maybe this is it. "One was always so deaf," she says quietly. "They didn't have these marvelous inventions in those days" — she fingers her gold hearing aid — "and I had to follow everyone around with my ear trumpet. I know I missed so much of what was going on."

The Manchester Gallery, where most of her paintings are hanging, is only about fifty yards away. I like her work better than I thought I would. The style is a curious, interesting kind of controlled primitivism, and she has always had an excellent color sense. There are a few sketches of Lawrence; and there is one large oil that shows a pallid, icy Lawrence drooping on a cross, while a satyr Lawrence, grinning with red lips and sharp teeth, offers him a handful of dark grapes. It strikes me as the kind of painting that Lawrence would have liked very much to do himself.

Bill and Rachel Hawk live up on Del Monte Ranch, on the Lobo, just as they did more than forty years ago when they were the Lawrences' neighbors and, for the first winter, their landlords. Lawrence and Frieda actually lived in the house that the Hawks now occupy, before they moved onto the land that Mabel Luhan gave them.

The Hawks have a lot of books on birds and animal life, and a black Persian cat that disappears when a stranger enters.

They have a quietness together, and a privacy. How many seasons here, with none of our time's myriad diversions for people who don't like each other? There is a long, old accumulation of affection in the Hawks' house — a kind of compound interest.

"No, I never found him especially attractive or magnetic," Rachel Hawk says. "I liked him, but the one I was really fond of was Frieda. She fought with him a great deal, of course — when they were living up here, we could hear them fighting all the way down at our house — but she had to. She was fighting back, all the time. She was a very strong woman, and very much alive, right up to the day she died."

Mention of Dorothy Brett makes her smile. "Brett," she says. "Well, Brett had this terrible crush on Lawrence, and finally Frieda got Lawrence to tell her that she couldn't live at the ranch, and that she wasn't to come up to the ranch more than twice a week. Well, she came every day. She'd ride around and leave notes on trees for Lawrence, or find someplace to hide and just watch him. You'd have to know Brett."

Bill Hawk listens, speaking up now and then: a small, wiry, attentive man with striking blue-green eyes. "I remember Lawrence came down once, asked me if I could take him on a pack trip right then, anyplace a way off. Said he just wanted to get away from those damn women." He laughs as though it had happened only a few days ago. "No, I couldn't take him. I had too much work to do at the time."

The Hawks remember how ill Lawrence was, and how he hated being ill. Frieda came to them once when he was spitting blood, and asked Bill to call the doctor. "Lawrence knew right away, and when she brought him in a tray of food he threw every plate at her, one at a time, and finished up with the tray."

In Mrs. Hawk's scrapbook are two cocoa-brown photographs of Lawrence on horseback, holding her son Walton on the saddle in front of him. For some reason, those two old pictures bring Lawrence closer than any reminiscence yet has: the familiar forms of hair and beard and trouble-ready mouth are a new reality by the separate reality of the boy. There was a Lawrence, after all.

I went to the Taos Public Library this morning and looked at books about Lawrence: thirty-four titles in a separate bookcase. The Three Fates all wrote books about themselves and him within a few years of his death. Their books have certain things in common — self-justification, self-blame, deep bitterness toward the others; and most of all, that sense of having secrets with Lawrence.

The same stories turn up in each woman's book, in each woman's version. Dorothy Brett cut Mabel Luhan's ear while trimming her hair, and writes that it was an accident and that she was sorry; but Mabel Luhan cries, ". . . she hated me, and she was deaf, and she tried to mutilate my ear!" Frieda claimed that Lawrence could not work without her, and that she actually wrote pages into his books. Lawrence often beat Frieda black and blue. Mabel Luhan and "the Brett" fought wildly over a painting of Lawrence's. Lawrence wanted his women to dress like his mother. There was a terrible, climactic evening when Frieda and a youth named Clarence were dancing together, and Lawrence and Mabel Luhan thundered around after them, crashing into them, and Dorothy Brett and her ear trumpet went round and round alone.

On the margin of a page in Mabel Luhan's book, *Lorenzo in Taos*, some exasperated reader has printed, "WHAT A LOT OF NUTS!" and someone else has added, "I AGREE!" Coming out of the library, I feel the same way. There was more of Lawrence in the Hawks' photographs than in all the books. The women's words screen out whatever joy there was, whatever glory, and let only the stupidity through, and the madness.

One dancer remains unclear still — Mabel Dodge Luhan, the woman who brought Lawrence to Taos. Her son by her first marriage, John Evans, still lives in Taos, in her old house. I called him this morning and asked if I could visit him. He sounded agreeable enough at first, but when I asked for directions to the house, he said shortly, "I'm sick of telling people how to get here. You sound like a bright young guy, and I'm sure you can find the way yourself." And he hung up.

A good reporter regards this sort of thing as a challenge. I have always hated challenges myself. I spend an hour or so hunting up and down the same street, and have to ask Louis Ribak to show me the road to John Evans' house. Then I set off, feeling intrepid.

The Evans house is in the town, within walking distance of the plaza, but it exists in a separate world, beyond old walls and high old archways. It is the center of a complex of houses that Mabel Luhan built and gave away over the years to friends — she seems to have had a phantom Rananim of her own.

There is a car in the garage, but no one answers when I ring the bell. I am rather relieved, truthfully; that was a strange phone conversation, and who wants trouble for the sake of Mabel Dodge Luhan? I ring once more before leaving, and the door opens. Mrs. Evans, a graying woman in a sweater and slacks, invites me in.

Her husband is asleep, so I talk with her for a long while. She seems cool and clear-headed and contemplative. She is a painter and a writer; under her maiden name of Claire Spencer she has published several books of fiction.

Mrs. Evans says that she liked her mother-in-law, and I believe her; but she speaks of her without liking, which is quite possible. "Mabel had one gift. She could size up people instantly, and know them — people she had never met before. Lawrence must have been like that, with that amazing perceptiveness. But she had no tenderness, none. For all the husbands, all the lovers, all the friends, she never cared for anyone. That was her tragedy.

"And she could never see a relationship between couples who

seemed to care for each other without trying to break it up. Lawrence and Frieda, Robinson Jeffers' marriage — my own marriage." She speaks calmly, always looking straight at me.

She sits on a couch, and I sit in a stiff armchair that resents me. She is telling how she and Mabel used to ride past Dorothy Brett's coat of arms, and how Mabel would invariably sniff and say, "How *vulgar* of the Brett!" — when John Evans comes into the room. I had almost forgotten about him. He is a tall, straight man with a really striking face: lean, mobile, dominated by thick black eyebrows and a mouth that seems tight and inexpressive until he speaks.

Whatever he may have said on the phone, he is obviously not going to talk about his mother and D. H. Lawrence, and he is already angry with his wife for doing so. "To what purpose do you want all that stale gossip?" he demands over and over. "To what purpose?" To make things worse, I'm sitting in his chair.

Mrs. Evans remains calm, but she seems to be retreating, growing smaller. When I say, "I think I'd better go," she insists that I stay for a drink. So does he, though to what purpose I can't imagine. She brings the drink and leaves us sitting in the living room, staring at each other and looking away.

"Uh, you must have been, uh, nineteen or twenty when Lawrence was living in Taos," I say to him I know damn well how old he was, and that he married a girl named Alice while Lawrence was there. It's all in Mabel Luhan's book. "That's right," Mr. Evans answers with a sour grin. "Uh, did you like him? What was he like?" Here's the seasoned journalist, the professional, on the trail.

Mr. Evans' smile seems to swoop at me, though in fact he has bent forward only an inch or two. "*Loathsome* man!" he says sweetly. "*Loathsome* man!" He draws the word out with a sound like the wind.

What a big drink this is. I want to go home. The funny thing is that I somehow like him. What is it I remember about him and Lawrence? Something in the book.

"Why are you picking over these old, old stories? It's old hat, the whole thing, it's been done and done and done. Who cares about it any more? You seem like a nice young man in your own right, and there are a lot of interesting young people in this town. You should be out talking to them, not to old crocks like me. Forget about Lawrence. Do something new, for God's sake, do something contemporary. Who cares about Lawrence?"

Here's the great journalist gulping his drink, mumbling, "Wellyoumayberight," and taking his leave: totally outmanned, outgunned, shot through the mizzenmast, stove below the waterline and listing badly to starboard. Mr. Evans says loudly, "Good-by — and take good care!"

"Of what?" asks the Spanish Armada.

"Of you!"

I lose my way looking for the front door. I knew I would. John Evans is right. I'm tired of this. I'm tired of poor, split Lawrence; tired of his gang of pitiful women who rubbed up against his genius like cats; tired to sleeplessness with piecing together the dim choreography of their sad ballet. The hell with it.

I remember what it was that I read in Mabel Luhan's book. She writes that before her son married, she asked Lawrence to have a talk with him about "whatever it was that needed to be said." So one night John Evans and Lawrence were closeted together for an hour; and when she asked John what Lawrence had told him, he replied:

> He said a lot. He said for me to be always alone. Always separate. Never to let Alice know my thoughts. To be gentle with her when she was gentle, but if she opposed my will, to beat her. And he said, above all, to be alone. Always.

She adds that from that time on there was no more rapport between Lawrence and her son.

Last night I took John Evans' advice in a way. I went to a reading by the Mexican poet Sergio Mondragon, and his wife Margaret Randall. Bob Sward introduced them, and afterward there was a party at the Swards' house. Except for Louis and Bea Ribak, and Margaret Randall's parents, the reading and the party were attended almost entirely by young people: students and what the newspapers call "nonstudents" when they make trouble — wanderers like the old goliards, all passing through Taos swiftly or slowly. I relaxed very gratefully with them.

Everyone I had talked to had read Lawrence's books, and most of them had a high respect for him; more than they had for Hemingway, say, or Scott Fitzgerald, two legends grown curiously distant in a short time, and perhaps less relevant to a young artist now than the legend of Lawrence. But they have their own mythology, their own ballads and sagas and folk heroes, their own prophets. They visit the shrine on the ranch, but they go as tourists, not as pilgrims. Their Lawrence is buried here.

Talking to Margaret Randall's mother at the party, I said, "I probably wouldn't have liked him." Her answer was both quick and thoughtful: "You would have liked him if he had wanted you to like him, I think."

Now, at the ranch, saying good-bye to the dead dancers *à la mode américaine* — by taking photographs — committing the casual sin of attempting to capture Lawrence's wild, wheeling, eagled view, I think of something that David Garnett said: that Lawrence had the gift of making things so visible that you could never again see them in your own way, only in his. What greater gift is there, in the end, for a man who wants to leave his mark on the indifferent mountains and the savage sky? His immortality is in them now. The rest is legend; the rest is ghosts and books.

The Poor People's Campaign

I: *The Southern Caravan*

They really were poor, by the way. People keep asking me about that, as though the depth of their own compassion depended upon it. It seems to be very important to ascertain that the members of the Poor People's Campaign, the muddy, ungracious dwellers in Resurrection City, were "representatives" — comparatively well-off messengers from the genuine poor back home. That's the polite way of putting it.

In a sense, it's true. The lost poor, the people long drained of the energy either for hope or for fury, for anything but staying alive — no, they didn't come to Washington. My friend Mr. Collins W. Harris, who owns the land he farms, and lives comfortably by the dire standards of Crenshaw County, Alabama, never expected it to be different.

"The people who ought to be with us, the ones who need help the most, they won't move to get it. You can't make them move. I know a woman down near where I live, she was born in a cowpen, and she lives there now, and she'll die in that cowpen. You couldn't get her to think about living nowhere else but there. In my community it's no good telling people how to do — you have to show them. You got to let them see you being what you talk about. So I just had to go on up to Washington."

But the people who did come to Resurrection City were properly poor, by the standards of anyone who is likely to be reading this story. I do want to get that cleared up. When in doubt as to the exact degree of deprivation, teeth usually provide a convenient index. Your true poor old man most often has a collapsed mouth: hard, slick blue-gray alternating with blazing splotches of infection; empty, except for a couple of tallowy lumps. The young ones — the girls especially — tend to have curved holes in the sides of their teeth, and soft bluish spots, almost transparent. They get sick easily, too.

Remember that poor people frequently lie about their condition, not only to reporters and interested visitors, but to one another. "How much money you think I got in my pocket right now? Yeah, well, I got as much as I need, man, as much as I need." The women will talk much more openly on that subject than the men and boys. The women's wounds are elsewhere.

'We eats grits and we drinks that Kool-Aid." she said. I never knew her name; she was a big old woman from Marks, Mississippi, who lost her shoes marching in the rain. "Grits and Kool-Aid and dry beans. I got my daughter and my three grandchirren living with me, and two of them little chirren ain't never had a piece of pork or a chicken in all they lives. My daughter gets fifty-four dollars and eighty cents a month from the welfare, and there ain't a job in town would pay her that much. It just seems like nothing every changes. For a while these few years, with Dr. King and President Kennedy and all, I was having some hopes that my grandchirren might be going to have a better life than I have had. But it just seems like nothing ever changes. When I was a little girl they wasn't no welfare, but sometimes you could kill a pig, eat pork all winter."

The Poor People's Campaign was born — partly, at least — out of those three desperate words: nothing ever changes. Dr. Martin Luther King, Jr., announced it last December as an extended program of demonstrations and possible civil disobedience in Washington, D.C. He spoke of "dislocating" the city, of tying up transportation, sitting-in at government offices, boycotting the schools, filling the hospitals and the jails — all the established methods practiced and perfected against the Bull Connors and Jim Clarks in such stations of the cross as Montgomery, Birmingham, Selma, Albany, Grenada, St. Augustine, in the days when the South was a lone, mad outlaw, and freedom meant voting and integrated restaurants. "These tactics have done it before," he said, "and that is all we have to go on."

But that was long ago, a generation. Then he had been able to compel the Federal government to protect the constitutional rights of Southern blacks; now he was calling for a revolution — for a guaranteed annual income, for the abolition of slums, for free food and medical care for the poor, for the creation of millions of meaningful jobs. In that one sad, foolish, lovely word, "meaningful," lay Dr. King's real radicalism, his challenge to a conviction as old as America: that the poor have no right to enjoy themselves. They may live, but they must never be allowed to forget that they are being punished. Dr. King's plan was to establish a grand coalition of poor people — black, white, Mexican-American, Indian and Puerto Rican — and to bring them to Washington in April: some 3,000 to begin with, and thousands more later. They would build a shantytown on public land (it was then to be called "The City of Hope"), and they would tell their story and be their story, making their need, their anger, their sickness and their beauty visible on the six o'clock news, day after day, for as long as it might take to shame a nation at dinner into seeing them. I don't think the plans were ever much clearer than that.

He spoke often of the Poor People's Campaign as the last chance to avert civil war and the fascist dictatorship that he feared must follow. But it seemed even then that he expected the campaign to fail, in terms of achieving its objectives, and that his real hope was to expose America's suicidal selfishness to itself and the world, beyond anyone's skill to cover again, or to forget. Reject these, tear down their shacks and run them home, and America will never again be able to lie about what it is. In no other country could that be conceived of as a victory.

On April 4, 1968, a few days before the Poor People's Campaign was to have been launched, he was murdered in Memphis.

The Reverend Ralph David Abernathy, Dr. King's closest companion and associate, succeeded him as the head of the Southern Christian Leadership Conference, and leader of the Poor People's Campaign. More beside than behind him stood a rank of brilliant individualists — Hosea Williams, James Bevel, Andrew Young, Jesse Jackson — all with more familiar names and flamboyant personalities than his own. Abernathy is a heavy man with a sad face. He may have been the best man Dr. King could have chosen as his heir, or the worst. I don't think it ever mattered.

The Poor People's Campaign was made up of eight contingents converging on Washington from different sections of the country. In early May I joined the caravan of buses coming up out of the deep South, starting from Edwards, Mississippi, and winding through Alabama, Georgia, the Carolinas and Virginia. The world of preachers and mules and tarpaper made to look like bricks — Martin Luther King's world. I was there for a little while in the summer of 1965. Everywhere else in the land, that was a generation ago.

The Southern Caravan was overwhelmingly black, of course. I

think there were eight whites out of perhaps 450 marchers. But in Fayette County, Tennessee, three summers ago, the only safety and comfort was to be surrounded by black faces, black shanties, broken black roads, to wriggle as deep down as possible into the body heat of the ancient black life. In a day or so, it was like that again, even to the difference in my voice; familiar, and yet altogether changed, forever. It is only my own stumbling hunger to be friendly that remains the same.

Sometimes there were eight or ten air-conditioned Trailways buses; more often we rode in tiny, stuttering crates with the names of high schools and Baptist churches painted on their sides. The black communities of each city we stopped in paid our way on to the next, as they fed us fried chicken, took us home to spend the night, and wished us a somewhat overeager "Godspeed." SCLC's taproot is the black Southern church, and the church can still command in Greenville, South Carolina, and get hundreds of box lunches fixed, and find money where there is no money. This is not the case in Chicago.

The oldest man I met was seventy-six, according to the middle-aged friend who was always with him. Toothless head as naked as a kneecap or an elbow; the flesh used up, fallen away around the high tendons — nothing left to him but bones, black skin, and a terrible sweet smile. I never heard him speak. The other man helped him to dress and undress, washed him, shaved him, talked quietly to him in the chaos of the church dinners and the rallies on the basketball courts.

"I take pains with him," he said. "Because I know God will bless me if I take pains with him." He was a tall, slow man himself, still strong, but starting to bend, starting to wear down. The two of them were next-door neighbors in Birmingham. "I got to carry him back home directly after we get there, cause he can't be sleeping out in no shack, his age. But he just wanted to go so bad. He's been real sick, too, with his stomach."

There were others nearly as old: women like huge, soft towers of starch; men as gristly as snapping turtles, their ages not measurable in years but in degree of defeat. But the majority of the Southern marchers were very young, ranging from junior high school age into the early twenties. Riding the buses with them felt like going off to summer camp. They drank peach wine openly, though it was forbidden, and stayed up all night fooling around the girls, and always had one more knife that they didn't turn over to the campaign marshals. In Fayette County they were like this — foolish, big-talking, blooming into unimaginable bravery.

Three years ago they were much more isolated, much less aware of other blackness, other poverty, other worlds. Now they know all about Watts and Hough and Rochester; about Chicanos boycotting the Los Angeles high schools and Dick Gregory going to jail with the Indians in Washington State — even about Harry Edwards' proposal that blacks refuse to compete in the Olympic Games. They knew about SNCC and Stokely even then in the southwest corner of Tennessee; but now, away down in Narks, Mississippi, they know who the Black Panthers are, and the Brown Berets. They aren't afraid of white people anymore, and they know that they frighten whites, and for a while this discovery will make all others secondary.

Wilson Talbert, a lean, neat nineteen-year-old from Selma, told me, "When I graduated from high school last year, I found there was just three kinds of jobs I could get. Porter, garbageman, waiter. That was it. That's all they got for black boys, stay in school or don't stay in school. They just gone draft you in the army, anyway, whatever you do. Ain't much to wait around for, is it? It used to be I didn't know to want anything better, but now I do. If I find a good job in D.C., I'm staying on up there — if not, I don't know. I'm not looking to get in no trouble, but you get to thinking about it, you don't know where to stop."

The young girls were in school or unemployed; most of the older women were on welfare. Grace Pitts, who got on the bus at Charlotte, North Carolina, is twenty-three years old, but she looks older, except when she smiles. She has a beautiful face, finely made and balanced, like a kite or a guitar. Grace is unmarried, but she has three children by two men. She lives on welfare, and such money as the oldest child's father gives her from time to time.

"I don't like being on the welfare. But we eat just the same food as when I'm working, so I think it's better for me to be home with my children. I know I'm not poor like some of these people" Collins Harris had chided her mildly for telling a reporter the amount of her allotment, which is three times what she'd get in Mississippi or Alabama — "but I'm poor. We aren't starving, but we don't ever get ahead, not one step. I'm going to Washington because I can't stand to think that it's never going to be any different. I know some of these women lived worse all their lives, but I couldn't stand it."

For all the new awareness, many of the marchers had never been more than fifty miles from home in their lives, and they grew homesick and fearful as the buses wound north. I remember a young man who stood up in the front of our bus as we neared Virginia to warn all the girls, "Look, sisters, from now on you got to be watchin yourselves all the time with these city boys, or you likely to wind up floatin face down in the river somewhere. I mean, we just play like we bad, but up here they ain't playin. You got to watch yourselves."

Henry Lee Williams had spent almost every day of his sixteen years in Marion, Alabama. Small, dark, square-faced, with shy eyes, he talked most of the time about a cafe where he loved to eat. He's known the woman who runs the place all his life, and she cooks the best chicken in the world. "You ever go down to Marion, you tell her you a friend of mine, and she probably charge you a little less. She don't cook just for the money, she's a real nice lady. I wish I was there right now, me and my friend Arthur."

I think it was in Charlotte that the rumor spread that everyone was going to have to make up five good reasons (some said ten) for going to Washington, in order to answer the reporters properly "when they come on the buses lookin for a fool." If there was such an edict, it was never followed through; but the story was believed, because SCLC was always doing things like that, or announcing them anyway. Rumors and official information proved accurate about the same percentage of the time.

At sixteen, Henry Lee is a veteran of the dogs and the jails, of being beaten up because it's fun. ("Every time that club miss my head, I hear it come down on the sidewalk — whock! whock!') He knew why he was going to Washington, but it panicked him to have to put it into words. This is what he came up with, finally, talking about his reason for dropping out of school.

"The books was all tore up. You be working on a problem, turn a page, and the next page might be gone, just tore right out. I couldn't work with no messed-up books like that. You know, a black student, he probably worry more than a white student about somethin like that, about not finishin a problem, spellin a word wrong. They take it very serious. You want to get it right, and sometimes you get mad."

The caravan's nurse, Nanny Washburn of Atlanta, rode on our bus. Reporters in every town always picked up on her, because she was white, and because her blind son was traveling with her. They used to describe her: faded and arthritic, eating her sunflower seeds and going on in a voice like a gnat, "America is a sick nation, so sick, and when the revolution comes we gonna have to put all them Congressmen in the mental asylum." No story ever mentioned that she had beautiful hazel eyes, luminous and perfectly clear: mermaid's eyes.

Nanny is a witness, Nanny is the Ancient Mariner. She was a labor organizer in Georgia in the twenties and thirties, when that was synonymous with being a Communist and a nigger-lover; in the endless Southern night, when nobody cared. There was no civil-rights movement then; there were no sit-ins, no boycotts, no movie stars buying full-page ads in the Sunday *New York Times,* no college students coming south for the summer, no federal troops in the schools, no voting acts in Congress, no cases before the Supreme Court. The Ku Klux Man flogged, castrated and murdered, and nothing was done, nothing was expected to be done. Nanny was there when nobody cared, and now she has no conversation: only a story.

She was frighteningly humble, this southern white woman who looks like my mother-in-law, and has been hit on the head with gun butts. "I want you all to tell me when I say something wrong or offend anybody," she was forever reminding us all. "I'm no intellectual, you know. I can talk to the people, cause I'm one of them, but you be sure and correct me when I say something stupid. I want you to correct me, cause I got so much to learn." Nanny Washburn, sixty-eight years old, with a dead husband, a blind son, and the blind daughter who died.

My best friend was Collins Harris. I don't know where he is now, or if I'll ever see him again. You might very easily have seen him in newspaper photographs, or on television: cameramen always zeroed in on him. Collins was the man wearing an old straw hat, the color of bottom-leaf tobacco, with a dark, frayed band around the crown that said FREEDOM. He had a white mustache, and a calm, solid way of standing still and looking around him. He turned fifty-eight in Resurrection City, but the dark brown skin was almost entirely unlined. Only his eyes were old; there were little skims of yellow in the white, and the outlines of the irises were beginning to blur. You would have remembered him.

We traveled together, sharing food on the bus, clothing when my knapsack got lost, and occasionally a bed — traditional American relationship between the white boy and the old black man. It is dying out now, with the world that produced it, and I wonder where the white boys will go to study competence and grace in the world.

Collins is a farmer, but he has made a living as a welder, a carpenter, and an auto mechanic. He has been married twice; he has children and grandchildren and children again, the last two adopted a few years ago. He shaves with a floppy straight razor. He believes in God, but not very much in ministers. There was a minister in Durham, North Carolina, who voiced some fear that the Klan might retaliate for his opening his church to the Poor People's Campaign. Collins was disgusted. "What's the use of a preacher who ain't got no more faith in God than that? That man got no business preaching to me."

He was with Martin Luther King from the beginning, the Montgomery bus boycott of 1955. Collins never talked much about Dr. King, just as he never sang or clapped during the marches, or applauded the speakers at the evening rallies. "I can't be bothered with singing lies," he said once. "I don't sing or pray less I mean it." But one evening in Norfolk, as part of the entertainment, a local boy got up and recited the "I have a dream" speech in a ghastly-perfect imitation of Dr. King's voice. I didn't like it then. I didn't realize what I was hearing. But when I turned to say something to Collins, he was crying, without making a sound.

As long as we were moving, it was all right. There were fights and hysterics, and every possible kind of logistical foul-up (buses and people got lost with the same ease as luggage); but even so, the spirit of the caravan was alive and hopeful. The best moment came when we marched five miles through Greenville and it rained so hard we couldn't breathe. The water was over our ankles, and we put our arms around the nearest shoulders and went on, laughing, gasping, pulling off our shirts, singing a dozen songs at once, totally disorganized but overcoming. The young man who led the march was a cripple on crutches, but he walked all the way, with two friends wiping the rain out of his eyes. They tried to make him get into a car, but he fought and cursed them so hard that they let him walk.

"We shouldn't have stopped for dinner," Collins said later that night. "We could have walked all the way to Washington." Then he laughed and nudged me, but I already understood that Collins is never just joking.

We never really got to Washington, not together. The Southern Caravan ended in Fairfax County, Virginia, nine miles from Washington. Resurrection City had been under construction only since May 13 — less than a week — and there was a shortage of food and housing for new arrivals. Our group was broken up and scattered through several private schools and Unitarian churches. We remained in those "holding centers" for three days.

It was a bad time. The momentum of the march was completely

dissipated; there was nothing to do but sleep, eat and watch television. Fights were popping everywhere, and people started being sent home in batches — worse, they began to leave on their own, out of boredom and homesickness. Robert Hanson, the crippled march leader, was robbed of all his money, and wept helplessly in the bathroom. "You try to be nice," he kept saying.

The SCLC staff who came out every day to hold the nonviolence workshops that were originally supposed to precede the campaign were as appalled by us as any white social workers might have been. From saying that we were the only people who could save the soul of America, they began to imply that we were being held in Fairfax County, not because Resurrection City wasn't ready for us, but because we weren't ready for Resurrection City. The character of SCLC — and the story of the Poor People's Campaign — is contained in that inversion.

They were afraid of our failing them, rather than the other way around. I think of the young SCLC girl — bright, pretty, certainly hip — who asked each of us in turn to give his or her definition of nonviolence, and refused to comment on the answers, or to reply to any questions herself, except with another question. Everybody got mad, and so did she finally. She snapped, "Look, I didn't come here to answer questions. I'm the one who's supposed to be asking them."

On the morning of May 22, ready or not, we were driven in private cars to Arlington Bridge. From there we walked to Arlington National Cemetery, to visit John F. Kennedy's grave. We sang "We Shall Overcome" very quietly, and stood silent for a little while, and then we walked back down to the bridge and over it into Resurrection City.

"Well, I'm home," Collins said. He was as calm and slow and easy as ever, but when he took my hand, his own hand was trembling.

II: Resurrection City

The rain wasn't what ruined it. The weather was dreadful, of course: not only during those three-day spells when the whole camp turned to a shimmering red-clay gumbo, but also in the brief intervals of dank heat that dried the ruts ankle-deep and sucked a sick, stinking fetor up out of the mud. Garbage wasn't collected; the truck that serviced the chemical toilets couldn't operate in the wet. It was cold, and there was nowhere to go to be warm. People stayed in bed all day, or sat by smoky trash fires. Mosquitoes actually started to breed in the flooded areas where the children liked to float around on big pieces of plywood.

But the rain wouldn't have mattered if the campaign had been moving. Boredom and confusion — not paid agitators from SNCC, as we kept being told — were the saboteurs of Resurrection City; but at the first flicker of direction, the slightest hint of real confrontation, the marchers surged together and functioned perfectly well. They picketed the Department of Agriculture in the rain, day and night; they spoke their minds to everybody from jumpy cops with two-foot billies to Attorney General Ramsey Clark; they went to jail for singing and praying in the streets on Capitol Hill. The SCLC leaders were annoyed about that, because it hadn't been planned in advance. Spontaneity made them as nervous as it did the Washington police.

It was all like a badly rehearsed ballet: a pas de deux between two strangers with no sense of each other's rhythms, ambition and limitations. There are moments of frantic improvisation, but what is happening is still a ballet, with rules, and an ending, and few echoes beyond that ending. Anyone who expected something different shouldn't have gone to a ballet.

Could it have been any different? — if Dr. King had lived, perhaps? Surely not in terms of what was achieved. I'm amazed that they squeezed as much as they did out of Secretary of Agriculture Orville Freeman: more money for the federal food stamp program; six new commodities added to that dole; emergency food distribution in about 250 poverty-stricken counties, and the standard programs established in 331 more. For this is Richard Nixon's sullen hour, and the Congressman's mail was running two and three to one against the Poor People's Campaign. It couldn't have ended any differently, but it didn't have to be the staged, dishonest mess that it was. Even with all that rain.

SCLC never truly decided just what Resurrection City was supposed to be. In the earliest rhetoric, it was going to be an instant slum, a deliberate embarrassment beside the beautiful Reflecting Pool. "We're going to bring all our troubles to Washington — all our lives and our rats and our roaches. . ." By the time we got there, it had been reconceived as a City of God, "where you don't pay no taxes, and you don't go to jail." At the end, it was an island. Nobody beyond the frail snow fence — and not everyone behind it — cared about Resurrection City.

Most of what the newspapers said was true; if they lied about some things, they missed a few others. There were guns in Resurrection City — I heard shots twice at night — and there were knives and a hell of a lot of liquor. Pot was easy to come by, and I knew at least one woman who was on heroin. There were rapes, shakedowns, attacks on tourists and reporters. Robbery was so common and unpunishable that most people quit bothering to report it. Of the marshals who patrolled the camp, half were thieves and bullies themselves, while the rest ran themselves almost insane without reward or encouragement. Dr. Abernathy and Hosea Williams kept on talking about those paid agitators.

Yet I never felt in danger in Resurrection City; and if I didn't love it, there were people who did. I remember a fierce man named Ray Robinson saying, "The moment I step outside this city, even just to walk over to the Reflecting Pool, I am dehumanized, man. Dehumanized. And I don't get human again until I'm back in Resurrection City with my friends. I have to make myself go outside, when I go."

Mrs. Mary Frances Thornton, a tiny, demure lady like one of those foot-high African antelopes, stayed on week after week with her ten-year-old son, though she hadn't meant to remain so long. "I like it here," she said. "There's nothing happening here that's any worse than Selma. I live in one room there, too, and it smells worse than anything in Resurrection City. Now here I've made some real good friends, and we're eating much better than we ever did in Selma, and nobody messes with me and Ernie. They talk about closing down Resurrection City, because of it being a health hazard and all, but nobody ever says they should close Selma down. That's what they should do, close Selma."

Most of the various contingents that came to Resurrection City remained more or less intact, settling into semi-independent city-states called "Boston," "Chicago," "New York," "Baltimore," "Philadelphia," and so on. The Appalachian whites were isolated in one swampy corner of the camp; the few hippies had their own quarter. Only the Southern Caravan was broken up, and many of the Mississippi and Alabama people were ill at ease among northern blacks. Young Henry Lee Williams was gone in a week, and Wilson Talbert left soon after. I don't think the two men from Birmingham — the old man and his friend — ever made it to Washington.

But a surprising number of men and women from the deep South hung on through the cold rain, the aimlessness and the trouble, walking round and round the Department of Agriculture; standing up in committee rooms to address polite, worried white men as distant as Martians; taking their food back to their shacks to eat in the quiet; sitting out in the sunlight on folding chairs, fussing leisurely for hours about some text in Matthew. They were home.

Grace Pitts and her children stayed to the end, and Nanny Washburn walked with her blind Joe wherever people were walking that day, passing out vitamins and saying, "It's wonderful, it's just wonderful. I'm just so glad I lived to see it." A half-crazy girl from Charlotte, whose fits of crying and fighting on the bus made her an immediate scapegoat for the other women, became something of a saint in Resurrection City when she stood up at a rally to announce that the welfare people wanted to take and put that loop inside her, so that she couldn't have any more children. "I got something wrong in me there," she said. "It's hurting me all the time, but I am not going to no hospital and let them doctors touch me and put that loop in me." Women started to cry, listening to her.

Collins Harris just went on being Collins Harris: unhurried, undeceived, yet everlastingly hopeful. Many things about Resurrection City distressed him, especially the ways of the northern city kids; but when I think of him, I see him ambling after a marshal who was dragging a boy in a gang jacket towards the plywood "City Hall," meaning to get him sent home. The point isn't that the boy hadn't done what the marshal said he had, and that Collins made the marshal turn him loose, but that Collins cared enough to move. He never seemed to think much about whether he should move or not.

Whatever he thought about SCLC's direction of the campaign, Collins remained completely loyal to Ralph Abernathy. Guerrilla talk bored him; boycotts, sit-ins, cooperatives and political pressure were his reality. "These kids running round hollering black power, black power, talking bad about everybody, calling Mrs. King 'Ol' Hattie,' I want to know where's they program? You got no damn program, don't you come bothering round me. I don't mind going to jail, I wouldn't care about getting killed, but not for no fools."

I used to watch him at meetings of the pointless, powerless, City Council, listening silently to furious monologues about how Detroit and Philadelphia got issued everything first, while New York, located a long way from the dining tent and out of earshot of the rickety public-address system, was having to buy and cook its own food, and we want our cooking gear back. The hippies would suggest that we live like our Indian brothers, in tribes, entrusting our decisions to those elders who were mystically connected to the old tribal wisdom. "I think we're getting too strung out behind this whole organization thing. Like that's the white man's bag, this categorizing thing." Council meetings went on like that for hours.

At last Collins would get up and talk one more time about the need for us to be like bits of sand and stone, mixing together into the common mortar of a new society. "If you can't be a rock, be a pebble, be a little chunk of gravel. It all makes mortar. I'm trying to be some cement, myself." I remember when he first came up with that image, studying an old brick wall. He loved good workmanship.

But there was no mortar in the Poor People's Campaign. Except for the Appalachian whites, none of the other delegations ever lived in Resurrection City. The Indians stayed in St. Augustine's Episcopal Church, the Mexican-Americans in the private Hawthorne School. Until very near the end of the campaign, we were told almost daily that our brown brothers were about to move in. We demonstrated with them a few times — at the Supreme Court and at the Department of Justice — but they weren't fooled.

"We have to read the damn papers to find out what you people are doing," a Mexican-American acquaintance told me. "And when we get something going by ourselves, you just walk right in and take it over, go home when you feel like it. We're having a rally or something, your guys come on and push our guys off the stage. Hell, we can't work with you, how we gonna live with you? You got no respect for us, no more than the Anglos, you think we can't tell?" Originally a triumvirate of equals — black, Indian and Mexican-American — was to make decisions for the campaign; but the closest that plan ever came to realization was an occasional hurried conference between Ralph Abernathy and Reies Lopez Tijerina, when the Chicano leader had been complaining too loudly about SCLC's domination. But SCLC never could share power much. I remember what a friend of mine who worked for SNCC in Mississippi said about them three years ago.

"They move into an area where we've been organizing, and it's like the circus coming to town. They won't work with the local people like we do — it's just a couple of rallies, a couple of speeches, couple of marches, a few heads busted, lots of headlines, and they're gone again, and we have to start all over. Nothing we can do about it, either. They got Martin the Ace going for them."

They don't have Martin now. One woman in Resurrection City said of Ralph Abernathy, "Dr. King could talk for twenty minutes, and I wouldn't understand one single word he said, but it didn't matter. Dr.

Abernathy, he talks for two hours, and I understand every word. But I guess I don't care."

His situation was tragic, but he kept finding his way into absurd, pitiable messes, caused mostly by a reluctance to trust his followers with the truth. The resentment engendered by his staff (and most of SCLC's people) living at the Pitts Motor Hotel might have been much less intense if Abernathy had simply explained that he couldn't possibly run the campaign from Resurrection City. But he let himself be acclaimed mayor, and he had volunteers — Collins was one — working every day on a big plywood house, which he never lived in. The low point came on the evening when he was called to the camp after there had been a couple of really bad fights. He promised sadly that if everybody got themselves together and behaved, he'd see to it that they got more fried chicken for dinner. Abernathy never made a speech in Resurrection City without promising chicken or filet mignon.

I don't want to hear any more speeches, not ever. The Poor People's Campaign ran on speeches, on metaphors, on slogans banged out over and over. Jesse Jackson's shouts of "Soul power!" and his morning ritual: "I may be poor, but I am — somebody! I may be hungry, but I am — somebody! I may not have an education, but I am — somebody!" James Bevel's signature image of white society as a dangerously sick, mad patient, and the poor as doctors and psychiatrists. Ralph Abernathy promising to smite the Pharaohs of this nation with plague upon plague, until at last they let our people go. And, always, the image of Martin Luther King Jr. as the murdered dreamer whose dream cannot be killed; as Joseph among his envious brothers.

> And when they saw him afar off, even before he came near unto them, they conspired against him to slay him. And they said one to another, Behold, this dreamer cometh. Come now therefore, and let us slay him, and cast him into some pit, and we will say, Some evil beast hath devoured him, and we shall see what will become of his dreams. . .

Hosea Williams, SCLC's direct-action leader, had the most striking image in his repertoire: the black dawn cities, with thousands of people hurrying way across town to haul the white man's garbage before he gets up, to start cleaning his house and fixing his meals; of mothers leaving their children to raise the white man's children. Hosea is the one who was always warning, "Tomorrow we are going to jail, brothers and sisters, tomorrow we are going to give the cops a chance to use those billy clubs. The picnic is over."

But it was never anything more than a ballet, a trivialization of real hunger, and real injustice, and real, sleepless pain. Now and then things flashed out of control for a moment, like the time a delegation from the entire Poor People's Campaign met with Ramsey Clark, having spent the previous day demonstrating outside the Department of Justice, demanding to see him. The grievance at issue was a Mexican-American concern, but the Resurrection City blacks took over, standing up one by one to sock it to Ramsey Clark just because he was there and white, and their lives are hopeless, and his department is unfortunately named.

Lila Mae Brooks of Sunflower County, Mississippi — where Senator James O. Eastland draws $13,000 a month for not growing anything on his land — shouted at Clark, "If we don't get no justice, man, you better be gone from here. You done sat down for too long. You done got fat back there. You letting the world know that you ain't a man."

Hosea himself was very quiet, murmuring only, "We ask justice to help us redeem the soul of America." But back in Resurrection City he chewed out Lila Mae Brooks and the other delegates furiously. Over and over he kept saying, "You got to ask the man for what he can deliver. I was ashamed of you today, shakin your finger at him."

But the day before, Hosea had been out there for seven hours, calling Ramsey Clark a criminal and a Pharaoh and a white god, and threatening to tear his playhouse down.

People like Lila Mae Brooks don't understand about ballet, about symbols, about the uses of rhetoric. They thought it was all for real.

In the evenings, now and then, I sat with shadows around the trash fires that gave Resurrection City the look of a Civil War encampment; or I drank sweet wine in a cold plywood shack, with the rain thudding on the plastic skylight. Somewhere around Baltimore, the kids would be beating on garbage cans, on bottles and motel pipes, drumming out the same rainy riff for five or ten minutes at a time, and then breaking flawlessly to a new phrase. There would be a candle glowing, and someone asleep in a corner.

"It's bullshit, brother, you know that. They ain't done nothin right since we got here, and it wouldn't make no damn difference anyway. Johnson ain't gone give us nothin that matters. No way."

'You hear they tryin to kill Abernathy?"

'Yeah, that would do it, man. I ain't sayin I dig Abernathy so much, but that would have to be it. Black power all the way then."

"I called my mama last night, and they ain't had one welfare check come in since I left there. Somebody said they was gone do that to anybody went to Washington, but I didn't believe it."

'Your mama! Willie Evans from Dearborn, his mama called home and she found out somebody had done ripped the roof right off her house. Just skin it right off, man, like you skin a banana. Just skin the whole roof off."

"God damn, they want it to happen! They want it to be the fire, and people gettin shot up and killed. And they gone get it like that, too — I don't see no way round it. I know it's comin."

A friend of mine called them the moribunds: the young men and women who are quite sure that they are going to be killed very soon. Many of them — wherever they are now — wonder often whether they will be able to shoot at their white friends when the time comes.

Cleveland Red, who might be seventeen or twenty-five, told me one evening that it was the Mafia behind all the trouble between black and white, behind all the trouble in the world. "We got to stop them, man, you and me. You telling me we gone let five thousand of them turn three billion of us around?" He never pretended to be nonviolent. "Shit, I been violent all my life, only I never called it that. You don't think about it, you just like a damn fish in the water. And they tryin to tell me about that Gandhi."

There was a lovely black girl from Newark who used to bounce up in front of me on the skiddy duckboards, demanding, "How are you today, my brother? How are you really holding out?" Her name was Dolores, and she had high cheeks and long, clean fingers. She was an astrology nut, and called everyone by his or her zodiac name. Once she said to me, 'Your race is finished, your time is over everywhere. I'm talking astrologically now, not politically. Even if you started to do right, it still wouldn't make any difference to the stars. Your cycle is over, that's all. Exhausted."

I liked her very much. I said, "Please don't call me *you* like that."

"I know, I'm sorry," she said. "But I have to do that, or else it just gets impossible."

On the night of June 4, Collins and I were roused in our shack (the soundest in our district, thanks to Collins' skill with a hammer and saw) by the rusty splutter of the public-address system coming to life. We came awake swearing — "Two in the damn morning, and they still playing around with that damn thing — " and then the words began to sink in. "Senator Robert F. Kennedy has been shot in Los Angeles. . ."

Robert Kennedy's murder marks a dividing line in the history of the Poor People's Campaign. In that week, Resurrection City's population — 3,000 when we arrived on May 22 — fell to about 500; in that numb and silent week, with a moratorium on all demonstrations, the last of the campaign's energy trickled away. When the demonstrations resumed, they had contracted to a 24-hour vigil at the Department of Agriculture, protesting Orville Freeman's refusal to recommend that food stamps be issued free of charge. It was at that time also that Ralph Abernathy was apparently forced by the SCLC staff to withdraw his support of Bayard Rustin as the organizer of the June 19th "Solidarity Day" demonstration. Sterling Tucker of the Washington Urban League replaced Rustin.

The Broadway and Hollywood visitors still came to Resurrection City, and that church money and assistance that only SCLC could have mobilized kept coming until the end. Living conditions did improve: electric lights, running water and sewer lines were installed, and a well-equipped day-care center constructed. But the sense of having been abandoned by the campaign leaders grew just as steadily. There were at least three invasions of the Pitts Motor Hotel by different groups from Resurrection City, demanding angrily that Abernathy and the others move out. They did at last, just before Solidarity Day, but by then it meant less than nothing.

They withdrew, little by little, not so much in the body — after all, they worked terribly hard, and stayed up all night holding conferences, and at the last Ralph Abernathy went to jail for twenty days — but in spirit. I'm an expert on the withdrawal of the spirit, and it has nothing to do with the activities of the body; in fact, there is often an inverse relationship. And the further away SCLC drew from embarrassing, hopeless Resurrection City, the more desperately they put on the messy people who stayed there. The saddest lie was the one about the "waves" of marchers all across the country, ready to move into Resurrection City if and when it was emptied by mass arrests. There was another about alternate camps being established in Virginia and Maryland.

There isn't much to say about Solidarity Day. Very few people knew who Bayard Rustin and Sterling Tucker were, but many — the young especially — sensed that the difference didn't matter at all to the

Poor People's Campaign. Dolores the astrologer said it early. "They'll make a jillion speeches, and sing 'We Shall Overcome,' and pledge to go home and work in their own communities. And then they'll climb right back on those buses. No, it's over, brother, all that sociable stuff. It's over."

Some 50,000 people showed up on June 19th, representatives of all the old alliances: the labor unions and the college students, the intellectuals, the clergy, the concerned middle class; Peter, Paul and Mary, Eartha Kitt. Hubert Humphrey made an appearance, and was booed. Eugene McCarthy was cheered. There were a jillion speeches, many of them quite good. But it was a very hot day, and there were few places where people could sit down and still hear the speakers on the steps of the Lincoln Memorial. By the time Ralph Abernathy spoke, it was nearly six o'clock — time for the buses to leave — and the crowd had frayed to 10,000 at most.

The night before, I had sat for a long time with four middle-aged black men on the raised porch that one of them had built in front of his shack, listening to a record of Martin Luther King Jr.'s speeches. Nobody said anything, but as each side ended they turned the record over to play the other again. I thought of that, listening to Abernathy.

"I intend to stay here until justice rolls out of the halls of Congress, and righteousness falls from the Administration, and the rough places of the Government agencies are made plain, and the crooked deals of the military-industrial complex become straightforward. . ." Dr. King was lucky to die when he did. It could have been him up there, telling lies with his heart breaking, instead of on that long-playing record in the night.

I left Resurrection City the next day. The camp's federal permit was due to expire on June 23rd, but I never thought the police would come in. I didn't understand ballet as well as I thought. Dolores's stars predicted it all, doubtless: not only Ralph Abernathy's big solo — the last march to the Capitol to be arrested — and the equally important ensemble of the thousand policemen stomping down the snow fence and flattening the shacks; but the kids throwing rocks at the cars cruising around their island, and the cops blanketing the place with tear gas at three in the morning. That wasn't part of the dance; but then classical ballet, classical theatre, isn't much in vogue today. They have this thing now where the audience gets up on the stage.

The last time I saw Collins Harris, he was adding a whole new section to the shack we had lived in for four weeks, to make room for more people. He had already made a table and a clothes closet, and he talked about putting in a little stove. When we said goodbye, he said, "Well, Pete, I enjoyed just about every moment we spent together, and the few I didn't, they wasn't your fault." I heard later that he got ten days in jail.

A BEAGLE BIBLIOGRAPHY

FICTION

A FINE AND PRIVATE PLACE (1960)
THE LAST UNICORN (1968)
THE FOLK OF THE AIR (1986)
THE INNKEEPER'S SONG (1993)
THE UNICORN SONATA (1996)
TAMSIN (1999)
A DANCE FOR EMILIA (2000)
FOR ALL WE KNOW (UPCOMING)

FOR CHILDREN

GORDON, THE SELF-MADE CAT (UPCOMING)

NONFICTION

I SEE BY MY OUTFIT (1965)
THE CALIFORNIA FEELING (1969)
AMERICAN DENIM: A NEW FOLK ART (1975)
THE LADY AND HER TIGER (1976; WITH PAT DERBY)
THE GARDEN OF EARTHLY DELIGHTS (1982)
IN THE PRESENCE OF ELEPHANTS (1995; WITH PAT DERBY)

COLLECTIONS

THE FANTASY WORLDS OF PETER S. BEAGLE (1978)
GIANT BONES (1997)
THE RHINOCEROS WHO QUOTED NIETZSCHE
AND OTHER ODD ACQUAINTANCES (1997)

SCREENPLAYS

THE DOVE (1974)
THE GREATEST THING THAT ALMOST HAPPENED (1977)
THE LORD OF THE RINGS (1978)
THE LAST UNICORN (1982)
SAREK — EPISODE OF STAR TREK: THE NEXT GENERATION (1990)
CAMELOT (1996)
THE STORY OF MOSES (1996)

PETER S. BEAGLE LIVES IN OAKLAND, CALIFORNIA. HIS UPCOMING NOVEL, *FOR ALL WE KNOW*, IS A MODERN RETELLING OF THE PERSEPHONE MYTH.